A Baby
for the Rancher

Margaret Daley

D0126849

HARLEQUIN® LOVE INSPIRED®

Special thanks and acknowledgment to Margaret Daley
for her contribution to the Lone Star Cowboy League miniseries.

Recycling programs
for this product may
not exist in your area.

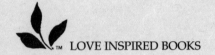 LOVE INSPIRED BOOKS

ISBN-13: 978-0-373-71939-6

A Baby for the Rancher

Copyright © 2016 by Harlequin Books S.A.

www.Harlequin.com

Printed in U.S.A.

If we confess our sins,
He is faithful and just to forgive us our sins,
and to cleanse us from all unrighteousness.
—*1 John* 1:9

To the other five authors in this continuity series. It was fun working with you all.

Chapter One

Sheriff Lucy Benson carefully replaced the receiver in its cradle, in spite of her urge to slam it down. Frustration churned her stomach into a huge knot. *Where is Betsy McKay?* None of her law-enforcement contacts in Texas had panned out. She'd been sure that Betsy was in Austin or San Antonio, the two largest cities closest to Little Horn in the Texas Hill Country.

Lucy rose from behind her desk at the sheriff's office. She grabbed her cowboy hat from the peg on the wall, set it on her head and decided to go for a walk. She needed to work off some of this aggravation plaguing her ever since the series of robberies had started months ago in her county. She still hadn't been able to bring in the Robin Hoods, as the robbers had been dubbed since many gifts given to the poor in the area had mysteriously started not long after the cattle rustling and stealing of equipment began.

Stepping outside to a beautiful March afternoon, she paused on the sidewalk and relished the clear blue sky, the air with only a hint of a chill. They needed rain, but for the moment she savored the bright sunshine as a sign of good things to come.

She was closer to figuring out who the Robin Hoods were. They were most likely teenagers who were familiar with the area and ranch life. Of course, that described all the teenagers surrounding Little Horn. But there also seemed to be a connection to Betsy McKay. The ranches like Byron McKay's were the main targets. The owners of each place hit by the Robin Hoods hadn't helped Mac McKay when he needed it. Could this be mere coincidence? Mac's death, caused by his heavy drinking, had sent Betsy, his daughter, fleeing Little Horn her senior year in high school.

The Lone Star Cowboy League, a service organization formed to help its ranchers, could have stepped up and helped more, although Mac hadn't been a member. But even more, Byron McKay, the richest rancher in the area and Mac's cousin, should have helped Mac when he went to Byron for assistance.

Lucy headed toward Maggie's Coffee Shop to grab a cup of coffee, and then she had to come up with another way to find Betsy. As she neared the drugstore, the door swung open and Ben Stillwater emerged with a sack. His Stetson sat low on his forehead, and he wore sunglasses, hiding his dark brown eyes that in the past had always held a teasing twinkle in them.

But that was before he had been in a coma for weeks and struggled to recover from his riding accident. The few times she'd seen him lately, his somber gaze had held none of his carefree, usual humor. He had a lot to deal with.

Ben stopped and looked at her, a smile slowly tilting

his mouth up as he tipped the brim of his black hat toward her. "It's nice to see you, Lucy. How's it going?"

"I'm surprised to see you in town."

"Why?" The dimples in his cheeks appeared as his grin deepened.

"You just got out of the hospital."

"Days ago. I'm not letting my accident stop me any more than necessary. I'm resuming my duties at the ranch. Well, at least part of them. I know that my foreman and my brother have done a nice job in my— absence. But I'm home now, and you know me—I can't sit around twiddling my thumbs all day."

For a few seconds, Lucy glimpsed the man Ben had once been, the guy who played hard and wouldn't stay long with any woman. He'd never been able to make a long-term commitment. How long would it take before he reverted to his old ways? Yes, he had been a good rancher and put in a lot of work at his large spread, but still, he had never been serious about much of anything except his ranch. And helping teens. "How's the Future Ranchers Program at your place going with your absence?"

"Zed and Grady have kept it going. I'd been working a lot with Maddy Coles, Lynne James and Christie Markham before the accident, so they knew what to do."

Maddy had been Betsy McKay's best friend while she'd lived here. Did she know where Betsy was and wouldn't say? "What are you doing in town?"

"Picking up my prescriptions. I had to get out of the house. I hate inactivity even if I have to work through some pain. I'm going stir-crazy, and I promised Grandma that I wouldn't go back to work until I'm home a week."

Again those dimples appeared in his cheeks. "What was I thinking? Only thirty-six hours, then I'm a free man."

"How's Cody doing?" She still couldn't believe that Ben was a father, although the DNA test that had come back could only state Cody was a Stillwater, a son either of Grady or Ben, identical twins. The eight-month-old was staying at the Stillwater Ranch, and Ben seemed to accept the fact he was the boy's dad since Grady had said the child couldn't be his. She'd always thought of Ben as a playboy, happiest with no ties to hold him down, but a baby could certainly do that.

Ben removed his sunglasses, his dark brown eyes serious. "A little man on the go. I think he knows the house better than I do."

She'd wanted to ask him about the letter, addressed to Ben, that she'd given Grady to give him. She'd found it in the wreck outside town where a young woman had died. Was she Cody's mother? What did it say? The words were on the tip of her tongue to ask him when she spied Byron heading for her.

Ben glanced at the tall man with a large stomach and wavy strawberry blond hair coming toward them. "He looks like he's on a mission."

"Yeah, I'm sure he is."

"Do you want me to stay?" Ben put his sunglasses on.

"No, he's my problem. You don't need the stress." The less others heard Byron's tirade the better she would feel. If she could escape, she would.

"But—"

"I mean it. Listening to him is, sadly, part of my job. Take care."

Ben tipped his hat and strode toward his truck, pausing a moment to speak with Byron, who frowned and continued his trek toward her.

"Sheriff." Byron planted himself in Lucy's path. "What kind of progress have you made on the thefts occurring?"

"I have a few leads I'm following."

"Like what?" he demanded in a deep, loud voice.

Lucy glanced around, wishing this conversation could take place in her office, not on the main street of Little Horn. "I have a possible lead on where the cattle are being sold. Without brands, it's harder to track the stolen cows." The rustlers had stolen new cattle that hadn't been branded yet.

"Yeah, we all know the thieves know what's going on here. Maybe when you find them, we should elect one of them sheriff next year when you're up for reelection."

Heat singed her cheeks as a couple slowed their step on the sidewalk to listen to the conversation. "That would be a brilliant idea. Put the crooks in charge."

"Sarcasm doesn't become you. I help pay your salary, and I want to see this settled. Now."

The drugstore door opened, and Lucy looked to see who else would witness Byron's dressing-down. His twins, Gareth and Winston, came to a stop a few feet from their father. Winston's eyebrows slashed down while Gareth's expression hardened.

Holding up a sack, Winston moved forward. "Dad, we've got what we need for the school project. Ready to go?"

A tic twitched in Gareth's cheek, his gaze drilling into his father.

The twins weren't happy with Byron. Lucy couldn't blame them. He'd been going around town, ready to launch into a spiel with anyone who would listen about what should be done to the rustlers and why she wasn't doing her job. His ranch had been hit the hardest.

Her gaze swept from one twin to the other. Maybe the boys knew where Betsy was. She needed to talk to them without their father. Anytime the conversation turned to Mac or Betsy, Byron went off on one of his heated outbursts.

Byron nodded at his sons, then turned to her and said, "Think about when you run for sheriff next year. Do you want me as a supporter or an enemy?"

"Dad, we've got a lot of work to do tonight," Gareth said in an angry tone, then marched toward Byron's vehicle across the street.

Lucy watched Winston and Byron follow a few yards behind Gareth; the middle-aged man was still ranting about the situation to Winston, whose shoulders slumped more with each step he took. Did those twins have a chance with Byron as their father? They were popular, but stories of them bullying had circulated; unfortunately, nothing she could pursue. It wouldn't surprise her because Byron was the biggest bully in the county.

With long strides Lucy headed again for Maggie's Coffee Shop. She needed a double shot of caffeine because she would be spending hours tonight going over all the evidence to see if she'd missed anything.

Ben Stillwater sank into the chair on the back porch of his house at his ranch near Little Horn. He cupped his mug and brought it to his lips. The warm coffee chased away a chill in his body caused by the wind. To the east the sun had risen enough that its brightness erased the streaks of orange and pink from half an hour ago.

Ben released a long breath—his first day back to work after his riding accident that had led to a stroke caused by a head injury at the end of October. He had gone into a coma, then when he had woken up, he'd faced a long road with rehabilitation. The accident seemed an eternity ago. He'd just discovered a baby on his doorstep, and he'd been on his way to Carson Thorn's house to figure out what to do when his world had changed. He couldn't believe months had been taken from him. An emptiness settled in his gut. He wasn't the same man.

So much has changed.

I have a son. Cody.

But who is Cody's mother?

He was ashamed he didn't know for sure. His life before the injury had been reckless, with him always looking for fun. Was the Lord giving him a second chance?

When he had come out of the coma, he didn't remember what had prompted him to go see his neighbor that day of the accident, a trip he'd never completed because his horse had thrown him and he'd hit his head on a rock. But lately he'd begun to recall the details. Finding the baby on his front doorstep. Holding the crying child. Reading the note pinned to the blue blanket with Cody's name on it. *Your baby, your turn.*

Grandma Mamie had told him in the hospital the DNA test had come back saying Cody was a Stillwater, which meant either he was the father or his twin brother, Grady, was, and Grady knew the baby wasn't his. The news had stunned him.

That leaves me. I'm a father.

He'd known it when Grady and Grandma had brought Cody to the hospital to meet him. In his gut he'd felt a connection to the baby.

Grady had gone into town, but the second he was back they needed to talk finally. One last time he had to make sure his twin brother wasn't Cody's father before Ben became so emotionally attached to the baby he couldn't let him go. And if Grady wasn't Cody's father, then that brought Ben back to the question: Who was Cody's mother? He should know that.

He sipped his coffee and thought back to seventeen months ago. He'd been wild before his riding accident. He'd worked hard, and he'd played hard. Not anymore. He had a little baby to think of. Lying in that hospital, piecing his life back together, he'd come to the conclusion he couldn't continue as he had before, especially because of Cody.

The back door creaked open, and Ben glanced toward it. Grady emerged onto the porch with a mug in his hand. Although they were identical twins, when Ben had stared at himself in the mirror before he'd shaved this morning, he'd seen a pasty-white complexion that had lost all its tan since he was in the hospital. His features were leaner, almost gaunt. A shadow of the man moving toward him with a serious expression, his dark brown eyes full of concern.

"I'm not sure I want to ask what's wrong," Ben said as Grady folded his long body into the chair across from him.

"Grandma said you were talking to her about Cody and his parentage. Are you having doubts you're Cody's father?"

"Are you?"

"No," Grady said in a forceful tone.

"I didn't really think it was your child."

"Why do you say that?"

"Because you're the serious twin. You're the one who does the right thing. I'm the rogue of the family. Everyone knows that. I was wondering more about who is Cody's mother. Sadly I don't know for sure. There's more than one woman it could be." Ben shrugged, then set his mug on the wicker end table near him. "Grandma said you had a letter for me."

Grady frowned. "She wasn't supposed to say anything. I was."

"I think y'all have waited long enough. I've been awake for weeks."

"Trying to recuperate from a stroke and head trauma. I didn't want to add to the problems you were facing with rehabilitation."

"I'm not fragile. I won't break, and I don't need protecting."

His twin started laughing. "You must be getting better. You're getting feisty and difficult." Grady reached into his back pocket and pulled out an envelope with Ben's name on it. "This is for you."

"Where did you get it?"

"The sheriff gave it to me for you."

"Lucy Benson? Where did she find it?" Why didn't she say anything to him the other day when they met in town? He intended to ask her that when he saw her.

"She found it on the front seat of a car involved in a wreck. The driver, Alana Peterson, died. There were also several bags with baby items in them on the floor."

Cody's mother was Alana? Ben had liked her and had had a lot of fun with her, but there had never been anything serious enough to lead to a marriage. He had a lot of mistakes to answer for. "When did this happen?"

"A week ago."

"You're just now getting around to it?"

"Yes." Handing the letter to Ben, Grady pinned his dark eyes on him and didn't look away.

Ben snatched it from his grasp but didn't open the envelope. If this was from Cody's mother, he would read it in private.

"Aren't you going to open it?"

"Later," Ben said while gritting his teeth.

"I know this is a lot to take in after all that has happened—is happening—but Chloe won't always be able to watch Cody."

"I figured when you two married she wouldn't be Cody's nanny for long. Y'all have your own life."

"She can for now, but she'll be having her own baby soon, and she wants to open a clinic. I want to see that dream come true for her," Grady said in reference to his fiancée, who was pregnant with her ex-husband's baby.

"She should have that clinic. She's been a great physical therapist to work with. I can't avoid doing my exercises each day here at home since she lives here. And I know you'll be a good father to her child."

"The ranch is going to be different with little ones running around."

"And not always the safest place for curious toddlers." Ben rose, stuffed the letter into his pocket and picked up his mug. "I've got a lot to consider. I'm meeting Zed at the barn." He started for the back door.

"I know we've had our problems in the past, but you've done well with the ranch."

Ben glanced at his twin and smiled. "Thanks. That means a lot coming from you."

As he entered the kitchen, he finished the last swallow of coffee and put his cup by the pot. He'd probably have more later, but he was eager right now to see the foreman. Zed had kept the ranch running while he'd been in the hospital. He headed for the front room where Grandma, Chloe and Cody were to see them before he went to the barn.

As he crossed the foyer, the doorbell rang. He detoured and answered the door, surprised to see Sheriff Lucy Benson. "What brings you out here? Did you catch the thieves?"

"Not yet, but I will. That's the reason I'm here." Lucy's furrowed forehead, intense green eyes and firm mouth shouted her seriousness.

Before his riding accident, a series of robberies had occurred, with cattle and ranch equipment and other items being stolen. When he came out of his coma, he discovered they were still occurring. The ranchers had been riled then, and now they were even more so, putting pressure on the sheriff to find the thieves with Byron leading them. "Sure, what can I do to help? Take on Byron for you?" He'd wanted to stay Wednesday afternoon, but Lucy liked to fight her own battles. She'd always been very independent and determined.

"Let's talk outside." Dressed in her tan uniform and cowboy hat, Lucy pushed the screen door wide to let Ben join her on the porch. As usual she was all business.

What would she be like off duty? Ben stepped to the side and waited for her to turn toward him, pushing that question from his mind. She'd always been off-limits to him. She'd made that clear when they were teenagers. "Is this concerning the thefts?" He stuffed his hands into his front pockets and encountered the letter Grady gave him.

"I don't know if anyone has informed you that your

ranch is one of the few big ones that hasn't been robbed yet."

He nodded, slipping his hands free. "Grady told me." He should ask Lucy about the letter, but all he wanted to do was forget he still needed to read it.

"I think somehow the robbers are connected to Maddy Coles or Betsy McKay, maybe both."

"I've been out of the loop. Why do you think that? Maddy is a great worker, and Betsy has been gone for almost a year, so how could she be involved?"

"After analyzing the ranches hit against the ones not robbed, I found a connection. Betsy McKay. People who were kind to her were spared. Then I took a look at who received gifts. Maddy did, including an iPod in her favorite color. That was a very personal gift, not the usual gift of animals or equipment the ranchers in need received from these Robin Hoods."

There was a definite divide among the people in the area because some of the poorer ranches were receiving help where they needed it, or at least they had until Lucy had started confiscating the nonanimal gifts. "It could be a secret admirer that gave Maddy the iPod."

"That's an expensive gift."

"Why are you focusing on Maddy? Others received gifts. Expensive ones."

"Maddy and Betsy were best friends. The ranchers who didn't help Betsy's father when he needed it were hit the hardest. Byron McKay, Mac's cousin, has been robbed more than anyone, and I think it might be because he refused to help his own family when Mac asked. Meanwhile, nothing has happened at this large ranch, one of the few left untouched."

"I can't see Maddy being involved in the robberies. Is that what you're thinking?"

Lucy took off her hat and ran her fingers through her short blond hair. "I didn't say she was. I said that there's a connection. The thieves have taken an interest in her. Why?"

"Do you think that Maddy working here is why we haven't been robbed?"

"It's a possibility. I have to look at this from every angle."

He wanted to help her. He imagined she wasn't happy with herself that these robberies had been going on for so long, especially with Byron spouting off to anyone who'd listen that Lucy wasn't doing her job. "What do you want to do?"

"What is Maddy's work schedule?"

"During the school year, she's out here after classes are over, for three hours. Then she comes for a full day on Saturday. The other interns, Lynne and Christie, have the same hours. They come and leave together. Before I was in the hospital, I often supervised them. I want this program to be a success."

For the first time, Lucy cracked a grin. "Yeah, I understand the intern program is your pet project."

Her smile transformed her pretty features and gave Ben a glimpse of her softer side. He'd been attracted to her in the past, but she'd made it clear she had no room for him in her life. Not that he could blame her. He'd never been serious about a relationship, and Lucy was definitely a woman who would want only a long-term one. He'd kept his distance.

"I'd like to hang around when they're here," she said now. "Maybe get to know Maddy better. I need to discover the connection between Maddy and the thieves. I might overhear something that will help."

"Won't the interns think it's strange all of a sudden to see you here?" Not that he wouldn't mind seeing more of the sheriff. He wasn't the same man he was before his injury. He had a son to think about.

"That's why I wanted to talk with you. I need a reason."

"We could pretend we're dating."

A blush tinted Lucy's cheeks. "Out of the blue? No one would believe that. Your reputation precedes you."

"I'm not that guy anymore."

One of her eyebrows hiked up. "Since when?"

"I could have died. That makes a man pause and take a good hard look at his life." He smiled. "It's not that far-fetched. I'm single. You're single."

"How about friends?"

"Getting to know each other?"

"I know you. That's the problem. When are you serious about anything?"

"I'm serious about my son, my family, the ranch and the intern program." He took a step toward her.

She moved back. "We don't have to say we're dating. You can be helping me learn about taking care of a horse. I might get one later."

"You've never had a horse?"

"My family didn't have a lot of money for that kind of stuff. You know that."

"Yeah. It seems I remember you occasionally would go for a ride with Grady and me when we were teenagers. Have you ridden besides then?"

Already tall, almost six feet, Lucy straightened even

more. "I've ridden. I had other friends who had horses besides you."

"Good to know you consider me a friend. Come tomorrow. It's Saturday. We'll go riding, and I'll show you what you need to do afterward with that horse, just in case you don't remember. That ought to give you a reason to hang around. Then we'll go from there. Okay?"

Her eyes gleamed as she gave him a nod. "I appreciate the help. If I don't catch these thieves soon, I'm going to have a lot of ranchers mad at me."

"Not me." He winked.

Her blush deepened. "That's because you haven't been robbed."

"True, but we could be."

"We haven't had any thefts in a month."

"See, you must be doing something right."

"I'm taking the nonanimal gifts away and keeping them as evidence for when I catch the thieves. I guess the Robin Hoods aren't too thrilled with that." Lucy finger combed her hair, then set her cowboy hat on her head.

"If they can't give to the poor, they aren't stealing from the rich?"

She started toward her sheriff's SUV. "It's that or something else, but I'm still going to find out who's behind this and bring them in. Just because it has stopped doesn't mean I'll stop pursuing them."

"Nor Byron McKay." Ben descended the porch steps. "I wouldn't expect anything less from you. I personally think you do a good job as the sheriff." Ben followed and hurried to open her driver's door.

Lucy chuckled. "You haven't lost any of that charm you're known for."

"My mama taught me manners, and since my grandmother is peeking out the front window, I need to make sure I keep those skills intact or…" Ben shrugged. "I'll incur Grandma's wrath."

"Smart man." Lucy slid behind the steering wheel. "What time tomorrow?"

"How about ten?"

"See you then." She gave him another smile, then started her car.

It will be interesting to see what she's like when she isn't being the sheriff.

Chapter Two

As she drove away, Ben kept his back to the house. He imagined his grandmother was still spying on him even though Lucy had left. Grandma Mamie had fretted over him ever since he'd come home from the hospital. If he had his hat that he liked to wear while he was working in the sun, he'd go on and walk to the barn to see Zed, who had stepped up into the foreman position when he was injured. But his Stetson was still on the peg in the hallway, which meant he would probably have to answer questions about Lucy's visit. Who was he kidding? Even if he didn't get his hat, his grandmother would interrogate him about Lucy's visit. He might as well get it over with.

As he strolled toward the front porch, he surveyed the pastures near the house. Several contained the horses they used on the ranch while one held their prized bull. They'd brought most of the cattle closer since the thefts started, but the barn and bunkhouse, where some of the cowhands lived, partially blocked the view.

As he entered his home, he spied Mamie in the doorway to the living room, holding Cody. Watching his son wiggle in his grandmother's embrace, Ben fought to suppress the laugh. Cody was going to be a handful. Already in the short time *his* son had lived with him, he was getting into everything he could reach when he crawled and used the furniture to stand up.

"I declare, this boy reminds me of you more each day. He doesn't like to stay still." Mamie thrust Cody into Ben's arms. "We're gonna be in serious trouble when he starts walking."

Ben swung him around, his laughter mingling with Cody's. "But he's got your stubbornness, Grandma."

She grinned. "That's true."

Ben peeked into the living room. "Where's Chloe?"

"She went to talk to Grady out back. I think they're trying to decide when to get married now that you're okay."

Ben kissed Cody's cheek, then held him against his chest, but the eight-month-old started wiggling again. "Okay, little man. You can get down until you get into trouble."

"Are you going to meet with Zed?"

Ben kept an eye on Cody as he crawled into the living room, heading straight for the coffee table and the few toys on the floor nearby. "Yes. With Cody living with us, I've decided to keep Zed in the position of foreman. He's been here the longest and has a lot of experience."

"I like that. He started out when your dad first ran the ranch."

The mention of his father made Ben clamp his teeth together before he said something he'd regret. His father had died a few years ago, but Ben could still hear the disapproval in his voice. Reuben Stillwater had been by the book, disciplined and serious like Grady, whereas Ben had taken after his mother. She'd divorced Dad when Ben was fifteen, and he'd become the focus of his father's anger. They'd always butted heads, but it had become worse, especially when she'd remarried after Ben turned seventeen. But while Grady had left the ranch to serve his country, Ben had stuck it out, trying to please his dad but never quite succeeding.

"He'd be proud of you, Ben. You've run this ranch well and increased the number of cattle we have, as well as the horses you're training for the rodeo. You even took his place on the Lone Star Cowboy League. Look at the intern program. That was all you."

"But whatever I did was never enough for him. At least I know how not to be a father."

"Remember, kids need boundaries, too."

"But love would have helped." And in the end his mother had left not only his father but him. She had been too busy having fun with her new husband until finally a skiing accident in the Alps had taken her life.

Grandma Mamie frowned, the wrinkles in her face deepening. "He loved you in his own way. He just wasn't a demonstrative man."

He wouldn't make that mistake with his son. Cody would know Ben loved him. "I need to get to the barn." Ben peered around his grandmother to make sure Cody was still playing with his toys. Then he clasped Grandma's arms and kissed her on the cheek. "But I'm glad I always had you, especially after Mom left." That day would always be carved with regret in his mind.

"I'm not surprised she left." A touch of bitterness laced Mamie's voice.

"She hated ranch life. She was happier traveling and

having fun with no worries." And forgetting about her two sons.

"That's true. When she married your dad, she never thought she would be stuck here all the time. Do you ever want to travel and see the world?"

Ben stepped to the peg and plucked off his cowboy hat. After setting it on his head, he turned toward his grandmother. "No, I love the ranch."

"It seems to me you have more of your dad in you than you realize, and Grady has more of his mother in him. He's the one who traveled and saw the world."

Ben needed this conversation to end. He strode to Cody, picked him up and gave him a hug. His heart swelled as he inhaled his son's baby scent and heard his giggles. Then he passed Cody to Mamie and headed for the front door.

"Have you read the letter yet?"

"No."

"Why not? Aren't you curious what Cody's mother had to say?"

"We don't know that for sure." *Alana Peterson.* He rolled the name of the woman in the wreck—Cody's mother—around in his mind.

"Then, why else did she write a letter addressed to you and have all those baby items in her car? Read the letter and find out."

He opened the door and glanced back at Grandma holding a content Cody. "I'm afraid to read it."

"You aren't afraid of anything. You'll try everything at least once."

"Not anymore. I'm a father now." He would not abandon his son like his mother had, or for that matter like his father, who had been there for him physically, but not emotionally. "I know he has you and Grady, but I want Cody and me to have a strong relationship. I want him to know I love him."

"Your dad loved you."

"He had a funny way of showing it. I'm not the same man I was the day I found Cody on our doorstep." And he did have fears, even if he didn't let on to others. He didn't want to end up like his father, bitter and alone, or like his mother, rootless and aimless. His examples of being a parent weren't the best, and he prayed he didn't end up like one of them.

Ben left the house and headed for the barn, his hand slipping into his pocket where the letter was. Mamie was right. He couldn't keep putting off reading what Alana had to tell him. He made a detour toward the corral near the barn and watched a stallion prancing around, showing off to the mares in the field nearby.

He leaned back against the railing and slowly removed the letter. He'd made a lot of mistakes in the past, and this short fling with Alana was one of them. He couldn't continue casually dating, never settling down. His son needed a mother, stability.

He opened the single sheet and read, his teeth grinding together. With a tight throat, Ben stared at Alana's words written in a neat handwriting.

"I tried being a mother. I just wasn't any good at it. I just want to have fun. You should understand that and not condemn me. I did some checking. I know your grandmother will help you. I have no one."

Those sentences jumped out at Ben. *How about me? I would have helped if you'd have let me know about Cody.*

Ben crushed the paper into a ball, then stuffed it into

his front pocket of his jeans. He remembered how he'd been before the accident, and he could see why Alana would say that. He'd always gone into a relationship with a woman knowing it was only temporary and casual. He didn't want to be responsible for another person's feelings. He'd already disappointed his father after trying for years to be the son he wanted. His mother, the one parent who he'd thought loved him unconditionally and accepted him for who he was, had left him, rarely contacting him because she was too busy building a new life with a new husband. And now she was dead and he had no chance of having a relationship with her.

He looked at the house, where his son was. He didn't deserve him, but maybe he could learn to be a good father, give him what he hadn't had with his own dad.

But not by living the way he had before. That was no life for a child. He needed at the very least a good nanny, or maybe it was time for him to get serious and settle down. Maybe in the future even marry. He had to change. He couldn't keep going down the same road. It led nowhere.

Where do I start? He felt lost and out of his depth. Then he remembered one of Grandma Mamie's favorite Bible stories about the prodigal son who finally came home, broken and humble. His father had greeted him with love and celebrated his return. Maybe it wasn't too late for him to reconnect with the Lord.

Lucy stopped by her small white house not far from Main Street to change from her uniform into more appropriate clothes to go riding with Ben this morning. She must be getting desperate to ask him if she could hang out at the barn when Maddy was working. But in her gut, she knew the girl and Betsy were somehow connected to the thieves. She needed results, and soon.

As a police officer in San Antonio for a few years before returning to Little Horn, she'd been a valuable member of several important cases. She wasn't alone in her frustration. The members of the Rustling Investigation Team of the Lone Star Cowboy League were aggravated, too. Their speculations of who the thieves might be weren't enough without hard evidence. In the past few months there had been enough accusations flung at certain people without any proof. That had divided her hometown. She didn't want to see that anymore. She needed hard evidence before arresting anyone, especially teenagers.

After changing into jeans, boots and a blue T-shirt, she headed to her personal car, put her gun in the glove compartment and drove to the Stillwater Ranch, bordered on one side by Carson Thorn's huge spread. She and Carson, as the president of the Lone Star Cowboy League, had been working closely to find the Robin Hoods. She always appreciated his counsel and was glad he finally was engaged to his high school girlfriend, Ruby.

Lucy parked next to the barn where other vehicles were, drew in a composing breath and climbed from her eight-year-old Mustang, purchased the first year she'd been a police officer in San Antonio. She'd always wanted to follow in her father's footsteps. She'd thought the action in a big city would prepare her for anything in the county when her dad retired from being the sheriff. But her hometown and rural county were very different from San Antonio.

As she walked into the long barn through the double

doors off the yard, two female voices came from one of the stalls on the right. Lucy spied a cowhand, not Ben, at the other end. She made her way to the girls cleaning out a stall.

Lucy stopped in the entrance, the scent of manure and hay overpowering. "Hi, Maddy. Christie. Do you know where Ben is?"

Maddy smiled. "He went up to the house but said to tell you he'd be right back." The two teenagers exchanged looks before Maddy added, "He mentioned y'all were going riding."

From the gleam in their eyes, Lucy wondered if Ben had implied something more about her presence here today. "Yeah, it's been a while since I've ridden. I don't want to get rusty."

"I can't see you forgetting how to ride. Remember you used to come out here when your dad visited mine, and we usually ended up riding."

Ben's deep baritone voice shivered up Lucy's spine. She glanced over her shoulder as he approached her. His cowboy hat, pulled down low, shadowed his dark brown eyes, but she knew there was a twinkle in them from the grin on his face and two dimples in his cheeks. He used to love to tease her when they were in high school. But then he'd flirted with all the girls. He would date, then move on, nothing long-term.

He paused right behind her—too close for her peace of mind. She held her ground. He'd reminded her that at one time they'd been friends, and he was giving her a chance to be here at the ranch and hopefully help her to get to know Maddy better.

Lucy slid her hand into her front pocket. "I remember, especially that time the bull got loose and nearly trampled me."

"I saved you."

"But you didn't latch the gate properly, and that's why the bull got out in the first place."

"It must be your dazzling smile that made me forget to check the handle was secured."

Lucy balled her hand in her pocket and forced a sweet smile. "I hope you've replaced that latch by now." The bull could be dangerous, but she decided Ben was more, especially when he grinned and focused his full attention on her.

"Right after you left. Is that why you never came back to ride?"

"It was traumatic, but I was leaving for college in San Antonio the next week and didn't have time."

"If it'll make you feel better, we don't have that bull anymore. But Fernando is probably twice as mean, so stay clear of him."

Behind her, whispers drifted to her, then one of the girls giggled. She was not going to blush. Instead, she jammed her other hand into her jeans pocket and curled it into a fist. "Thanks for the warning."

"Our horses are saddled and out the back door. I need to see Zed for a few minutes, then we'll leave. Maddy and Christie, why don't you show Miss Benson around since it's been a while. We've expanded the barn since you were a teenager."

Lucy wanted to hug Ben and stomp on his foot. He could be so aggravating and accommodating at the same time. He was giving her time to establish a rapport with Maddy. "That would be nice."

The tour was brief, consisting of a walk-through of

the barn with a hand wave toward the tack room near the front entrance and Zed's office closer to the back one. Most of the horses were in their corrals. When Lucy stepped outside with Maddy and Christie, she noticed two horses saddled and tied to the fence. Maddy pointed out the various paddocks and pastures nearby besides explaining which animals were usually in them.

"Do you all enjoy working here?" Lucy asked, hoping the girls would forget she was the sheriff in time. "I once thought I might train horses, but then I was only ten and soon decided I wanted to be a nurse until I realized I would have to give people shots. I hated shots. I couldn't see myself doing that." It hadn't taken her long to realize she'd really wanted to follow in her father's footsteps, and now she was.

"I want to train horses, and Saul has been working with me and showing me what he does as a trainer since Ben's accident. Before that, Ben was training me." The wind caught Maddy's ponytail and it danced about her head.

Christie shrugged. "I get school credit working here. Dad wanted me to learn about ranching, so I signed up for the work program. Since I can't participate in Future Ranchers at our own place, this is a good choice. Ben is a great boss."

"Yeah, we hated what happened to him." Maddy glanced behind her. "I've fallen off a horse, but thankfully I didn't hit my head on a rock like he did."

"Me, too. I broke my arm when I was twelve," Christie said.

"Isn't there a third girl who works here?" Lucy asked as Ben walked toward her.

Maddy brushed stray strands of her hair, caught in the

wind, from her face. "Lynne is out working with Emilio and Josh mending fences."

Ben joined them. "After lunch, y'all will go out there with Lynne. Thanks for showing Lucy around."

The mention of lunch made Lucy's stomach rumble. She should have eaten her usual big breakfast, but she'd spent the morning catching up on paperwork, which was still not finished, and only managed to eat a hard-boiled egg and drink two cups of coffee.

When the teens strolled toward the barn, Ben swept his arm toward the two horses tied to a fence railing. "Ready?"

Something in his voice, a catch on that one word, caused her to look at him more carefully. "Are you all right?"

"I just realized this is the first time I've been able to ride since my accident. It's not as if I haven't been thrown from a horse before. I rode broncos in the rodeo, and I came close to really being injured several times."

His confession took her by surprise. He'd never shown her a vulnerable side before. In fact, she'd thought he'd never been bothered by much. "I once was pinned down in a shoot-out in San Antonio. I didn't think I was going to get out of there. I was out of ammo, and all I could do was pray to God."

"He answered your prayer?"

"Yes. It wasn't a minute later before the gang realized I didn't have any more bullets, but backup arrived."

"I think what's different about this time is that I have a son now to think about. With his mother dead, I'm his family."

"How's Cody? Chloe has kept me informed about him."

A grin lit his face, forming those two dynamite dimples in his cheeks and putting a gleam in his dark eyes. "Into everything. I walked early. I would be surprised if he doesn't in the next month or so."

Ben had a great smile, and when it was coupled with his charm, she could see why women were attracted to him. "And you were probably climbing everywhere."

Ben chuckled. "Yep. When I was eighteen months, my mom once found me on top of her tall dresser. I used the drawers as steps."

The familiar sound of his laugh warmed Lucy. When she'd seen him in the hospital the first time, she'd wondered if she would ever hear that again. "Do you remember doing it?"

"Nah. Mamie has told me a couple of times this week when warning me about Cody." He started toward the smaller horse. "I'll give you a leg up."

Lucy lifted her left foot into his connected hands, getting a whiff of his lime-scented aftershave as he helped her mount. Her heartbeat kicked up a notch, only because she hadn't gone riding in a while. It had nothing to do with the man accompanying her. They were just friends.

When Ben sat on his black stallion, he paused and looked around.

Beneath the shadow of his hat, Lucy glimpsed a neutral expression. She couldn't read anything in it, which was unusual for Ben. "Are you okay?"

Then he grinned. "Just deciding where to ride. I thought about heading toward Carson's ranch, but Thunder was the horse that threw me, so going that way might not be the best choice for my first time in the saddle in months."

"How did your accident happen?"

"I was preoccupied about finding Cody at the ranch and didn't see the snake until it was too late. Unfortunately Thunder saw it and reacted. I'm just glad the rattler didn't bite me when I was on the ground unconscious."

"God was looking out for you."

"You think? Lately I've been wondering if the Lord was giving me a wake-up call. I know I attended church with the family, but to be honest, I've never been that serious. I needed to be shaken up. I have a child now." He pulled his rein to the right and started toward the dirt road in front of the barn.

"You're serious about changing?" Lucy had known Ben forever and only saw him as the charming ladies' man that he'd been for the past fifteen years.

"I'm working on it. When I woke up in the hospital, I knew that I had been given a second chance, and this time I don't want to blow it."

Lucy had seen others say they were going to change, but they never did. It wasn't an easy thing to do. Habits were hard to break—and human nature even harder.

"Chloe told me riding would be good for me. Help me get stronger. I feel like a weakling and, you know," he added, swinging his attention to Lucy, "we macho men don't like to be weak." Then he winked at her.

Laughter bubbled to the surface. "You're incorrigible."

The dimples deepened as he touched his brim and nodded once. "I aim to please. I'm feeling cautious today. Let's go toward Tyler's ranch."

She rode next to Ben along the road passing by the older original barn. He stopped in front of it. "I'm thinking of hosting a young cowboy/cowgirl camp here this summer and using this barn. It's still in good shape but a distance from the house, so not used as much."

"Didn't your granddaddy move everything to the new location?"

"Yeah. Grandma Mamie still comes once a month to weed the garden she had at the old house. Zed, who lives here, is thrilled she does. As tough as he tries to be, he loves the flowers that bloom in the garden. He told me once coming home after a long day and seeing those bright colors always lifted his spirits."

"Maybe Mamie would come over and plant a garden like that for me. Of course, she'd probably have to take care of it. I barely have time for housework, let alone yard work."

"Zed and you aren't the only ones who love bright colors. Cody almost got hold of the flowers in a vase on an end table. Thankfully I managed to grab him in time." Ben urged his horse to move forward.

Lucy fell in beside Ben on the road. "Your son is named after your grandfather. That couldn't be a coincidence. Are you Cody's father? Is that what the letter I gave Grady from Alana was about?"

All evidence of a smile disappeared. "Yes."

"I'm sorry Cody's mother died in the car accident. Was she coming back for him?"

Ben's mouth turned down, his posture ramrod straight. "No, she didn't want Cody. I'm just glad she left him at our ranch and not somewhere else."

Tension poured off Ben for a long moment, and Lucy wished she hadn't brought up the subject of Cody's mother. She knew that Ben's mother had walked away from her marriage and sons. She rarely had come to see them before she died. Was Ben thinking about the correlation?

She wanted to change the subject. Never before had she and Ben had deep conversations, and all of sudden they were talking about the past. "How far along are you with plans for the camp?"

"Before my accident, I'd been talking with Carson about it. I wanted the Lone Star Cowboy League to sponsor the camp as an outreach project. Last week before I came home, I told him I was still interested in doing it. We'll be getting together about it soon, since the camp could start in June, if we have the time to do it that fast. There will be a lot to do in three months. It'll be something my son will enjoy when he gets older."

She slanted a look at Ben as he headed across a field behind the old barn. She'd never thought of Ben as father material. This side of him was interesting, but would it last? Like a hummingbird, he'd flit from one flower to the next, never staying long.

Chapter Three

Sitting around the large table in the kitchen, Lucy still felt shell-shocked. She hadn't intended to stay longer than necessary for her job. The horse ride had been over an hour when she'd thought it would last maybe thirty minutes. And now she was eating lunch with the family. How had she let Ben talk her into staying? He was lethal when he turned his full-fledged smile on her. But in her defense, she'd been starving, and riding the mare had only increased her hunger.

Yes, that's it. Not Ben's charm.

But then she looked across the table at Ben. A hard knot in her stomach unraveled. He was feeding Cody, who sat next to Ben in his high chair, and she had a front-row seat to watch. His baby giggled, grabbed for the spoon and flung some sweet potatoes into Ben's face.

Lucy pressed her lips together to keep from laughing. She couldn't hold it in and joined the rest at the table while Ben patiently took his napkin and wiped it off his cheek.

"Good aim, son. I guess you aren't hungry anymore."

"I always say when a child starts playing with their

food, they're finished." Mamie grabbed the plate while Ben went for the spoon in Cody's hand.

But the baby was too quick, and the utensil sailed halfway across the table, landing in the middle of the pasta salad.

Ben moved the high chair back a little so Cody couldn't get hold of anything else to throw, then took a bite of his turkey sandwich.

Lucy turned to Chloe. "See what you get to look forward to. Food fights."

Chloe chuckled. "Cody is definitely preparing me for my own child."

"When are you due?" Lucy took a swallow of her sweetened tea.

"Three months and counting. That's why," Chloe said, glancing at her fiancé, Grady, "we've decided on a small wedding this month with family and close friends. I don't want to be a whale waddling down the aisle."

"Never, not you." Grady leaned toward her and gave her a quick peck on her cheek.

"Just let me know when to show up," Ben said, accompanied by a wail from Cody.

But as he turned toward his son, Mamie stood and took the crying child out of his high chair. "He usually takes a nap after lunch. Almost like clockwork. I was afraid he wouldn't last since we held lunch. I'll be right back."

"Grandma, I can take him to his room." Ben started to rise.

His grandmother waved him down. "Nonsense. You have a guest here." Then she scurried unusually fast for a seventy-eight-year-old woman.

Ben watched them leave, then faced the three remaining at the table. "I know everyone has tried to fill me in on what I've missed while I was in a coma and the hospital. Besides the crime spree with the Robin Hoods, anything else you've forgotten to tell me other than the letter you gave me *finally* yesterday morning?" He stared at his brother.

"I'm pleading ignorance." His mouth twitching, Grady took a sip of his drink. "I was gone for two months of that. You'll have to depend on Chloe and Lucy to tell you."

Everyone peered at Lucy. She held up her hand. "Why are you looking at me?"

"You're the sheriff, and you know everything," Ben said with a grin.

No, she didn't. What had been in that letter from Cody's mother? "Other than six months of robberies and now nothing, that's it. It's been pretty quiet, thankfully."

"Carson finally proposed to Ruby. They are engaged, and it was about time. I thought they would marry in high school." Chloe reached for the pasta salad and took the spoon from it before dishing up more on her plate. "You know the saying. I'm eating for two."

"And Eva and Tyler got married. I'm glad our cousin and Tyler are together." Grady stood and took his plate to the sink.

"Yes, and I hope they'll adopt a baby," Mamie said as she came back into the kitchen. "Eva was really good with Cody and would make a great mother."

Lucy finished the last bite of her sandwich. "I guess the biggest surprise was Amelia and Texas Ranger Finn Brannigan. I never saw her falling for another Texas Ranger. Funny how things work out."

"You should never say never. I've found it comes back

to bite you." Ben retrieved a wet dishcloth and wiped down the high chair. "I never saw myself as a father, and I wake up from a coma to find the baby left on our doorstep is my son."

Lucy almost asked Ben why he didn't think he'd ever be a dad, but she didn't. She knew about the shaky relationship he'd had with his own father, but from what little she'd seen today, Ben was trying hard to be a good one.

"Another surprise was Clint falling in love with Olivia. He'll be an instant dad to triplets when they marry in June." Grady refilled his iced tea.

Just weeks ago Clint's father's remains were found in the Deep Gulch Mountains, where he'd met an accident years ago. Clint hadn't been abandoned like he'd thought. "The nice thing is Clint now has closure about his dad leaving him when he was a child. I think he'll be able to relate to Olivia's boys."

"Lucy, what happens if you can't find out who's stealing from the ranchers?" Ben retook his seat across from her.

"I'm going to." She was up for reelection next year, and if she didn't find the persons responsible, Byron McKay would probably put all his money and community presence behind getting a new sheriff.

"The Rustling Investigation Team thinks it could be teenagers," Grady said, covering Chloe's hand resting on the table.

Ben threw Lucy a look. "Is that really why you want to hang around the barn? I thought it was my irresistible charm."

"Like I *already* told you, Betsy McKay is connected somehow, and Maddy was her best friend. I've talked

with her as the sheriff before today, but she was wary.
I didn't feel that way earlier." She was not going to let
Ben get to her.

Chloe's forehead creased. "You think Maddy and
Betsy are robbing the ranchers?"

"We've tried to find Betsy but haven't been able to
locate her. But no, not Maddy. I did some checking, and
she has an alibi for one of the robberies. She was at a
sleepover with four other girls. She may know something
and not realize it." From what she'd seen and heard about
the foster child, she was a good kid.

"So this is why you asked the league for a list of members with teenagers," Grady said.

All eyes turned to Lucy, and for a brief moment she
felt like a suspect being interrogated. "Yes. As we have
surmised, the Robin Hoods are probably two or more
teenagers, most likely boys based on the equipment
they took. The thieves would have to be strong. Neither Maddy nor Betsy fit that profile. The Robin Hoods
would have to be comfortable around cattle and horses
to take them without anyone knowing. They would also
have to be able to drive a trailer and be familiar with the
area around here."

"That describes most of the teenage boys in the vi-
cinity. I see why you want that list." Ben shifted his attention to his twin. "I understand Tyler is going on his
honeymoon soon. I'd like to take his place on the Rustling Investigation Team. We need to find whoever is
doing this."

Grady shook his head. "You've only been home
awhile, Ben. You're just getting your strength back."

Ben drilled a hard gaze into his brother. "I know what
I'm capable of. Do I have to go to Carson about this?"

"No." Grady glanced toward Lucy. "If you want to take Tyler's place, then do, but don't forget you were in the hospital for a long time. You don't have to do everything the minute you are released. I was going to sit in for Tyler, but you can instead. I have to go to the VA in San Antonio for a couple of days next week. The team is meeting Wednesday night. Lucy, is that okay with you?"

"Sure." Oh, great. More time she'd be spending with Ben. She placed her napkin on the table. "Thank you for inviting me to lunch, but I have paperwork to finish at the office, so I'd better leave."

Ben's grandmother grinned. "I'm so glad you could join us. Don't be a stranger."

"I'll walk you to your car." Ben rose at the same time Lucy did. She shouldn't be surprised he'd said that because Ben was always a gentleman.

Outside, Lucy set her cowboy hat on her head and slipped on her sunglasses. Ben strolled next to her without his Stetson. When he paused next to her car, he squinted, the wind catching his sandy-brown hair that touched the collar of his plaid shirt.

He took her hand. Lucy started to pull it away when she spied Maddy and Christie standing just inside the barn doors looking at them.

"I thought we decided *not* to play that game," she whispered while giving him a sweet smile.

"We're not playing any games. You are a friend, aren't you?"

She nodded.

"I'm thanking you for a nice ride this morning. I didn't think about falling from my horse once while on Thunder. It must be the company I was keeping. Will I see you before Wednesday night?" The volume of his voice rose enough that the girls probably heard the question.

"At church tomorrow?"

"I'll be there. But I thought you'd want to go on another ride before the sun sets after work next week."

"How about next Wednesday? I'll come early, maybe go for a ride, then go to the meeting?" The things she did to get to the bottom of this investigation.

"Sounds like a date." He quirked a grin and squeezed her hand before releasing it and opening her driver's-side door.

As she drove away from the ranch, she glimpsed Ben saying something to the two teenage girls, then heading back to the main house. Tall, he walked with confidence, but he'd lost weight while in the coma. But that wasn't the only thing that was different from before. There was something in Ben's bearing that had changed. Maybe because he was a father now.

Lucy entered Maggie's Coffee Shop and spied the owner behind the cash register. Maggie Howard had been a few years ahead of her in school and had always been a kind and generous woman. Lucy smiled and waved at the petite redhead, then scanned the café for Chloe. Lucy saw her and made her way toward one of her best friends. Although Lucy's job as sheriff took her all over the county, Little Horn would always be her home and base. She'd discovered when she lived more than six years in San Antonio that she was a small-town girl at heart.

"I'm glad you could meet me for lunch," Chloe said to Lucy as she sat down.

"It sounded important."

"We finally decided last night what we want for our

wedding. Pastor Mathers will marry us at church, and then we'll go back to the ranch for a small gathering of family and friends."

Lucy knew about all the problems Chloe had had in her first marriage and her ex-husband's unfaithful behavior, and was thrilled her friend had found someone who would be a good dad for her unborn baby. When Chloe's ex-husband had heard he would be a father, he'd wanted nothing to do with the child. "When is it?"

"In ten days on Friday evening. The wedding will be at six and the dinner at the ranch at seven."

"I hope I'm invited, or I'm going to crash your wedding."

"Of course, you are. I want you to be my maid of honor. The only people at the church will be Mamie, Ben as best man and you."

The waitress stopped at the table to take their orders.

After she left, Lucy leaned forward and asked, "What can I do to help?"

"The beauty of a small wedding is there won't be much to do. The cook at the Stillwater Ranch and Mamie are going to plan the dinner. So all you have to do is show up at the church." When the waitress set their drinks on the table, Chloe paused, then said, "Are you dating anyone?"

Lucy dropped her jaw, then snapped it closed. "Why?"

"Just wondering. The last time we talked about men I was going through a divorce and you weren't dating anyone, but you've been at the ranch a lot lately. Interested in Ben?"

"It's police business." Lucy sighed. "Are you going to be one of those women who because she's deliriously happy thinks everyone around her should be in a relationship?"

"What's wrong with that? I want my friends to be happy."

"You forget I tried a serious relationship in San Antonio. Jesse didn't work out." That was putting it mildly. She and Jesse had been talking about getting married until she'd stumbled across a woman he was dating in Austin when he went there for work. Then to make it worse, he had begun taking out another lady in San Antonio while professing the whole time he was in love with Lucy. "The men I've seen and dated have a commitment phobia. I'm usually around two kinds of men— law-enforcement officers and criminals. Neither have I found to be good husband material."

"Your father has been married to your mom for thirty-eight years. Every time I've seen them when they visit you, they're still in love as though they are newlyweds."

"My dad is the exception." He was nothing like Jesse, the FBI agent in San Antonio who'd stolen her heart and stomped on it. But besides Jesse, she'd also seen fellow officers on the San Antonio police force she'd worked with either drink excessively or date excessively. When they did marry, the marriages usually didn't last. She didn't want that for herself.

"Do you find it hard to follow him as sheriff?"

"Lately I've felt I'm letting people down."

Chloe waved her hand. "Stop right there. That's Byron McKay talking. He's never happy about anything."

"He has been hit hard by the cattle rustlers I can't seem to find."

"That isn't your only case. You take care of everyone

in the county. Remember the robbery in the next town? You caught the guy within twelve hours. And when that toddler went missing six months ago? You found the two-year-old within hours."

Lucy chuckled. "Okay, you've made your point. But reelection is next year, and I want to continue my dad's legacy."

"You are."

Abigail set the plate with a chef salad in front of Lucy, then gave Chloe her order. "Can I get y'all anything else?"

"No, this looks delicious." Chloe dug into her hamburger immediately. "Mmm, and I wasn't wrong."

Abigail grinned. "I'll tell Maggie. She loves to hear her customers are satisfied." The waitress left, hurrying toward the kitchen, her long black ponytail bouncing with her strides.

Lucy glanced around. Every table was occupied, which was usual at this time of day. When the door opened, she caught sight of Ben entering. He scanned the coffee shop.

"Ben!" Chloe held her arm up. "You can join us."

Lucy chewed her bottom lip as Ben threaded his way through the crowded café. She always looked forward to her girl time with Chloe, but she couldn't blame her for signaling that Ben should sit with them. Chloe would be his sister-in-law in ten days, not to mention she was taking care of his son.

Ben removed his hat and set it in a vacant chair and then took the last one at the table for four. "I keep forgetting this isn't a good time to come to Maggie's, but I thought I would grab something to eat before heading to see Pastor Mathers."

"You've been out of action for a while. That's understandable." Chloe popped a french fry into her mouth.

Ben peered at Lucy, his gaze penetratingly warm. "You're still coming to the barn before we go to the meeting tonight?"

She nodded and speared some of her lettuce, trying to ignore the quickening of her heartbeat at his perusal. "I want to spend time with Maddy, Lynne and Christie. I find when teenage girls get together they gossip. I might overhear something that will help me." That was the easiest way for her to get a glimpse of what was going on with the teenagers in Little Horn. She still felt two or more were involved in the thefts. At twenty-eight, Lucy was the youngest sheriff to date for the county, but she would stand out at school, so her undercover work had to be somewhere else.

After Abigail took Ben's order, Chloe retrieved a couple of five-dollar bills from her wallet. "This is for my lunch. Cody will be getting up from his nap, and I need to be there. I've been gone all morning to the doctor."

Ben pushed the money toward Chloe. "Keep it. My treat. Is the baby okay?"

"Right on target. In three months, she should be here."

"Grady is excited and can't wait." Ben took his mug of coffee from Abigail and drank a long sip. "I'll be back after I meet with Pastor Mathers."

Chloe stood. "Are you going to be at the barn, then?"

"Yes, but I can always be reached by cell. Thanks, Chloe, for staying on as Cody's nanny. It's hard being a single parent, and I've only dealt with it for a brief time."

"I love being with Cody. It's good experience." Chloe headed for the exit.

Ben turned his full attention on Lucy. She felt he

was assessing her in a new light. "Did you enjoy Pastor Mathers's sermon on Sunday?" she asked, hoping to divert his focus.

"It's made me think about what's my purpose. I never really thought about it other than taking care of the ranch. But we're more than our job."

Lucy couldn't really say that. "My work is my life. It requires long hours and being willing to go out to a crime scene in the middle of the night."

"Do you have to do that often?"

"Lately, more than usual. If a serious problem arises, I need to be available."

"Twenty-four/seven?"

She nodded and focused on eating while Abigail delivered a roast-beef sandwich to Ben. "I want to be involved. That's the way my father was. By the time he retired, he knew most of the people in the county. That fact helped him numerous times besides knowing the terrain. I think some of the stolen cattle are being kept somewhere nearby, but I don't have the manpower to cover every square inch."

When her cell phone rang, she snatched it off the table. "Sheriff Benson."

"There's a robbery in Grafton. 214 Second Street. The feed store," the dispatcher said.

"I'm on my way." Lucy rose as she withdrew her wallet.

Ben shook his head. "My treat. See you tonight. If you can't come to the ranch beforehand, let me know, and I'll meet you at the Lone Star Cowboy League center."

"Thanks." As Lucy left the coffee shop, she glanced over her shoulder, and her gaze instantly connected with

Ben's. Again her heartbeat picked up speed, and she hastened outside before she did something crazy like blush.

Ben entered Little Horn Community Christian Church and hurried toward Pastor Mathers's office. When he'd called Ben to set up this meeting, Ben had wondered why. He almost felt like a child being called to the principal's office, but he and his family had attended this church for years. He might have doubts about his faith, but the pastor had come to the hospital every week and prayed for him. Grandma Mamie had been certain he'd regained consciousness and recovered faster than the doctors thought possible due to all the prayers being sent up in his behalf, led by her and Pastor Mathers.

Ben spied the pastor in his inner office. The man waved to him to come straight inside.

"I'm so glad we have a chance to talk." Pastor Mathers skirted his desk and stretched out his arm.

Ben shook his hand, then sat where the man indicated on a comfortable-looking brown couch against a wall. "I enjoyed your sermon Sunday."

Pastor Mathers took his seat at the opposite end of the sofa. "I was glad to see you at church. It's been months. I know how concerned your grandmother was, but our prayers were answered."

It took all Ben's willpower not to squirm on the leather cushion. He'd never felt comfortable talking about his feelings, and he certainly didn't know his purpose in life. "Is there something you needed to see me about?"

"Yes. This year is the Stillwater Ranch's turn to hold the children's annual Easter-egg hunt and celebration. I told your grandmother we could skip your ranch this year because of your injury, but she wants to do her part.

I know you're still in physical therapy and with having been away from the ranch for months, you have a lot to catch up on, so I thought I would ask what you think. I don't want to put too much on you. The community will understand if you pass. In fact, Carson offered his place so don't feel you have to."

"Are you kidding? It's a big, fun celebration for the kids. I love helping with that event even when it's not at my ranch, and now that Grady is home there will be two of us." He and his brother hadn't really talked about if Grady was staying in Little Horn or not, but Ben hoped so. Right before Grady had left for his last overseas assignment, they had gotten into a huge argument, to the point he was surprised to see Grady when he woke up from his coma. Their relationship was still strained, but there was hope it would heal. He'd been thrilled when Grady had asked him to be the best man at his wedding this morning.

"If you're sure, then I'll add you to the planning committee. Their first meeting was in January. I know every year you've helped with any extra activities like races. It's always been a highlight, but I didn't know what kind of restrictions your doctor has put on you."

He remembered his neurologist had told him under no circumstances was he to participate in any bronco competition or a similarly dangerous activity that would cause him to be thrown from a horse repeatedly. If he hit his head like he had, he probably wouldn't recover. "I won't be doing anything risky. I have a son to think of now. No more things like riding a bronco in a rodeo."

As he said that to Pastor Mathers, Ben was beginning to understand how Grady felt with his war injury. For years they had never had much in common except a last name, but maybe at least his head trauma would bridge the gulf between him and Grady.

Pastor Mathers nodded. "I understand. I know how much you've enjoyed working with children, so I believe you'll be a wonderful father."

Ben was glad the pastor thought that, because he felt as if he'd been thrown into deep water without the ability to swim. But the one thing he knew was that Cody was quickly becoming the center of his life. All his son had had to do was smile at him that first day Mamie and Grady had brought him to the hospital for Ben to see and hold him.

"Maybe next year you can think about being a helper with the youth group."

"Me?"

"Sure. I think you'd be perfect."

How? His attendance at church was sketchy, and he wouldn't call himself an overly religious man. "I'll think about it."

"No decision needed until August, but there will be at least one vacancy at that time."

Ben left the church, his mind in turmoil with thoughts racing through it. Ever since he'd started having the teenagers at the ranch in the intern program, he'd been looking for other ways to help the young people in the community. He wanted to give them chances he really hadn't had. And now the pastor was asking him to help with the youth leader. Him! He wasn't the most likely candidate, and the request had stunned him.

Ben drove through the main gate at Stillwater Ranch, still trying to decide what he should do. He couldn't accept it if he wasn't the best person for the job. *God, what are You telling me?*

After he parked near the house, he went inside to check on Cody before going to the barn. The urge to hold his son swept over him. He'd never thought of himself as father material, but in this case he didn't have a choice, and he wouldn't do a job unless he could do it well.

He entered the house through the kitchen and headed toward the front room, where most of the family congregated. The large window afforded a beautiful view of the family's horses in a pasture, the bluebonnets starting to bloom and poke their heads up through the sea of green grass.

Cody's giggles floated to Ben. He hurried his step. When he paused at the entrance into the room, he honed in on his son grasping the cushion of the ottoman. Then he began pulling himself up. When he stood, Cody let go of the cushion but didn't take a step.

"When did he start doing this?" Ben asked Chloe, who sat in the chair with the ottoman.

"I'm as surprised as you are. He's always holding on when he stands."

Cody gripped the edge and then with one hand tried to reach for a ball he loved to play with. He wobbled, then plopped back onto the floor. Ben moved closer to watch his son again drag himself to a standing position and try to grab the ball—just out of his reach. Cody stood on his tiptoes and his chubby fingers grazed the red plastic toy. It rolled away. Finally he burst out crying and fell down.

Ben scooped Cody into his arms and rocked him. "You're okay. Before long you'll be climbing up on that ottoman."

Cody slowly calmed down and looked at Ben, touching his face. Ben kissed his fingers, then swung him high. His son's laughter resonated through the house.

"I wish I could stay and play, but your daddy needs to get to work. See you later, little man."

Ben sat him on the floor by his toys, plucked the red ball off the ottoman and rolled it to Cody.

"Is Grandma here?" he asked as he straightened.

"She's taking a nap."

"Is she sick?"

"Just a little tired. Cody apparently didn't stay down for his nap as long as he usually does."

"Thanks, Chloe. I'll be at the barn."

As he walked across the yard, he realized he had to find at the least someone to take Chloe's place. It wasn't fair to Mamie to think she could take over full-time when Chloe wasn't available. Maybe even a woman he was interested in. He needed to look beyond just a nanny for his son. Cody needed stability. He'd been shuffled around enough. He'd checked and found that Alana had left Cody with her aunt for a month before dropping him off at the ranch.

When he stepped through the double barn doors, no one was around. Zed should be back soon with the interns and cowhands. They were rotating the cattle to another pasture. A noise at the other end turned his attention in that direction. Suddenly a hunched figure, wearing baggy sweats and a hoodie, raced out of Zed's office midway down the long center aisle toward the back door.

"Can I help you?"

The person increased his speed and darted outside.

Ben rushed after the trespasser. Was this one of the thieves? Had he taken anything? Ben reached the yard behind the barn and glimpsed the guy climbing over a fence. Ben went after him, his breathing labored, his muscles protesting the exertion. As he scaled the fence, the person put more distance between them.

Perched on the top railing, Ben realized the futility of trying to pursue the intruder. He hadn't regained his full strength. Something that would have been easy six months ago wasn't anymore. After catching his breath, he retraced his steps toward the barn, wondering why that person had been in Zed's office. Had the thieves started robbing again?

Chapter Four

❧

Ben entered his barn, his body protesting his mad dash after the intruder. Still winded, he inhaled deep breaths and came to a stop as Lucy appeared in the doorway at the other end. A smile brightened her face when she looked at him and headed toward him.

As she drew closer, tiny lines crinkled her forehead. "Is something wrong?"

"I'm not sure." He slid a glance at Zed's office. "There was someone in here. When I came in, he walked out of there, saw me and raced out the back. I'd say that's a big red flag."

"Did you recognize him?" Lucy moved toward the office. "Did he have anything in his hands?"

"He wasn't carrying anything. He was dressed in a dark hoodie, and about all I could say was the guy was slim and about five feet eight inches."

"But you think it was a male?"

"Yes." Ben removed his Stetson and ran his fingers through his hair, finally beginning to breathe normally. "At least by the way he walked and his body build." He followed Lucy into the room, which had a desk and chair.

His gaze fell on the chart of the layout of his ranch that took up almost one wall.

Lucy stood near the desk, examining the contents on top. "Do you see anything out of place?"

"You'll have to check with Zed for sure, but the computer, printer, phone and my rodeo championship trophy are all here." He crossed to the computer and switched it on. "You have to enter an access code." After typing it in, he checked a couple of folders. "I'll have Zed go through it more thoroughly, but I don't think the intruder messed with it."

"Okay, then why in the world did someone come in here for nothing and risk getting caught?"

Ben turned his attention from the focal point, the desk, and surveyed the rest of the office. After he tried the file cabinet, he said, "It's still locked. Zed keeps it that way when he isn't in here." As he continued his inspection, his gaze latched on to the three teenage girls' belongings on the floor behind the door.

A stack of all the Harry Potter books in the series were tied together with a red ribbon, and on top of them was a silver music box with Maddy's name engraved on it. He gestured at the gifts. "I can't image Maddy bringing these in here. She would leave them in the car with her backpack."

"Do you think the intruder left them?" Lucy leaned down and lifted the lid on the music box with a pencil. Her eyes widened.

Ben stepped nearer, getting a whiff of Lucy's light flowery scent as he stared at the silver necklace with a horse charm dangling from it. "Whoever gave this to Maddy, he has good and expensive taste. None of these presents are cheap."

Lucy turned her head and peered up at him, so close he glimpsed the light sprinkle of freckles on her pert nose. She opened her mouth to say something, but no words came out. Instead, their gazes embraced and held.

Voices out in the barn disrupted the moment, and Ben quickly straightened. Lucy stood, a rosy hue on her cheeks, and put some distance between them.

"Let's see what Maddy does when she sees the items." Lucy sat in a chair while Ben lounged back against the desk, his hands gripping its edge.

"Hi, boss," Zed said as he entered the office. "We just finished moving some cattle to a new pasture."

"Did Maddy, Lynne and Christie help y'all?"

Zed nodded. "I'm gonna hate to see them go at the end of the school year."

"Me, too. I'm thinking of hiring a couple of teens for the summer months."

Zed looked at Lucy. "Are you two still going riding?"

With a glance at the clock on the wall, Ben shook his head. "I guess we both got delayed. We have to be at a meeting in an hour." Shifting to Lucy, he grinned. "Can we have a rain check on that ride?"

"Sure."

Lynne knocked on the open door. "I need to get something from my jacket."

Ben swept his arm toward the area.

As the teenager stuck her hand into her coat pocket, her attention fastened on to the gifts on the floor. She bent over to read the engraved name, then popped back up and hurried from the office. "Maddy, you need to see what you got in here."

Ben exchanged looks with Lucy while Zed asked, "Where did those come from?"

Ben shrugged. "Maybe Maddy knows."

"I know what?" The girl paused in the entrance, her view blocked by the door.

"About these gifts." Ben pointed toward them.

She spied them and squealed, stooping by the books and picking up the music box. When she opened it, her jaw dropped. "Who would do this?"

Lynne and Christie leaned around the door. "You've got a secret admirer, Maddy. Probably the same one who gave you the iPod," Christie said and whistled.

Maddy blushed. "Ben, can I put these in the car?"

"Yes. You don't have any idea who gave you these beautiful gifts?"

"No, sir. But I love them, especially the necklace. I don't have a lot of jewelry." Maddy rose with the books and music box and hurried out of the office with her two friends right behind her.

Lucy walked to the doorway and peered at the girls leaving out the front of the barn, giggling and whispering.

Ben came up behind her. "What do you think?"

"She seems genuinely surprised, but do you really think she doesn't know who is giving her the presents?"

"Yes. In all my dealings with her, she has been very straightforward."

"What happened here, boss?"

Ben pivoted toward Zed. "I chased an intruder out the back of the barn. I didn't see who it was, but he came out of your office. I think he left these gifts."

Zed's bushy eyebrows shot up. "Well, I'll be."

"Has Maddy said anything about a boyfriend?" Lucy moved into the office as the sound of the girls returning floated on the air.

"No, but then I don't think they would be gossiping when I'm around." Zed tossed his hat on a peg and sat behind his desk. "Just a reminder, the girls are only staying another half an hour. They have their monthly Future Farmers of America meeting tonight."

"I'd forgotten about that." Ben drew Lucy out of the office and took her hand, then strolled out the back. "I want to show you where the intruder fled."

Lucy peered over her shoulder at the three teenagers parting and each disappearing into a separate stall. When they were around the corner and out of sight of anyone in the barn, she tugged her hand free from his. "The show is over."

"What show?" he asked, pressing his lips together to keep a straight face while Lucy tried to control the flush staining her cheeks.

"You keep insisting on acting as if we're a couple."

"Me?" He pointed to his chest, then chuckled. "Lucy, it's the most logical reason for you to be coming to the ranch and hanging out with me at the barn."

Releasing a long breath, she shook her head. "You're certainly persistent. I'm going to have to find someone for you to become interested in."

"How about you come tomorrow afternoon? We can go for a ride, then have dinner."

She opened her mouth.

He knew she was going to say no, so he hurriedly added, "Once a month Grandma has the girls come up to the house after work and have dinner with us. She doesn't believe they eat enough. I think she's trying to put some pounds on their bones. It's always the day after the FFA meeting."

"How does your grandmother do everything? She's

always got something going either here, in town or at church."

"Talking about church, as you know I met with Pastor Mathers today. It's Stillwater Ranch's turn for the big Easter-egg hunt."

"So you told him you'd host it this year?"

"Yes. I always enjoy it. I think I'm a kid at heart."

She laughed. "You won't get an argument from me. So I guess you're coming to the next meeting at church about the Easter-egg hunt?"

"Yep. Why?"

"Because I'm chairing it this year."

He stared at her. "Where do *you* find the time to do everything?"

"Good question. I don't sleep." One corner of her mouth lifted. "No, seriously, I like to stay busy."

"Well, so do I, but I also find time to play. Lately, it's been me playing with Cody."

"He's a cutie. What are you going to do when Chloe has her baby?"

"I don't know. I'm working on it. But let's get back to the question of coming for a ride and dinner tomorrow night. Are you coming?"

"First, I wasn't the one who sidetracked the earlier topic. You were. Second…"

When she paused for a few seconds, he hurriedly said, "It'll help keep up the charade we're a couple in the girls' eyes."

She frowned, looked toward the barn, then at him again. "*Charade* is a good description of what this is because we are *not* a couple."

He loved to rattle her. "It's still the best way for you

to hang around here. So should I tell Grandma we have another one for dinner tomorrow?"

"Yes, now show me where the intruder went. Since it's been so dry, I doubt there are footprints, but maybe the tide is turning on this investigation and we'll get fingerprints."

Ben started for the fence. He wanted the Robin Hoods found like everyone else, but it sure was fun having Lucy hanging around his ranch.

At seven o'clock, Lucy pulled out of the parking space in front of the Lone Star Cowboy League building. "Since you're replacing Tyler on the Rustling Investigation Team, at least tonight was a good time to get you caught up on what has been happening since the end of October."

Ben angled toward her. "The only promising lead is where the cattle possibly are being sold, if not in Texas."

"Yes, the Oklahoma State Police are working on it from their end. I've also contacted New Mexico."

"If they are being sold in Oklahoma or New Mexico, then how could it be a couple of teenagers? If they were gone several times to sell the cattle, they would have to be away for at least a day. I could see it once, but to move the number of cattle they have stolen, it would be four or five times. Wouldn't their parents realize something is going on?"

"Kids can get creative. Some parents would, but others don't keep track of their teenagers like they should."

"What if the teenagers are working with someone else to sell the stolen cattle? Maybe they aren't leaving but that person is."

"Once we find the place we think the cattle are going,

we'll be able to figure out if there are more people than the Robin Hoods involved. But having a middleman makes sense. You think that person could be from around here?"

"Maybe. Maybe not. Let's grab some hamburgers before going home." Ben pointed at the Hamburger Hut at the end of Main Street.

Lucy slanted a glance at him. During the meeting, Tom Horton and Amanda Jones, other members of the team, had been giving Ben and her quizzical looks. But then she couldn't blame them. Ben sat close to her and even once had put his hand on the back of her chair. "Frankly, I'm surprised Amanda didn't ask me after the meeting if you and I were dating with all the attention you gave me. Is this dinner in public to continue your rouse we're a couple?"

"We aren't even getting out of the car. They serve us curbside. But no, I'm starving and trying to put some weight back on."

Lucy chuckled. "That's not a bad problem to have. Not having to worry about what and how much you eat."

"The key to the diet is being in the hospital and rehab for months, not even doing half of what you're used to."

Although Ben's tone was light, teasing, Lucy parked at Hamburger Hut and shifted around. "Dieting is never easy, but that isn't the way I would want to lose weight. How are you doing? Really?"

"I wish I had the energy I had six months ago. I'm glad Grady is still at the ranch to help me otherwise…" He sighed. "I'm not sure what I would do."

"You're doing quite a bit."

"Yeah, with the help of an afternoon nap. A couple of days ago Zed found me napping in the hay. I didn't even have the energy to go back to the house and lie down. If nothing else, my accident showed me not to take anything for granted. You'll never know when it will be taken away."

The wistfulness in his voice touched Lucy. He was right, and it took incidents like what happened to Ben to reinforce that. "Good advice."

"Hey, don't sound so surprised. Occasionally, I can be serious."

"What do you want to order?" Lucy asked as she studied the menu and decided on her usual.

"The hamburger platter special with a vanilla milk shake and water."

Lucy placed their orders, then relaxed against the seat for the first time that day. "I like their platter special, too. I wish I could have the milk shake, but iced tea will have to do. What time do you want me to come tomorrow?"

"The interns work from three to six, so anytime you can after three. We'll eat shortly after six."

"Four." Which meant she would go to the station early. She wouldn't want Byron McKay to accuse her of slacking off on her duties.

"I'll have Maddy show you how to saddle your horse."

"I've done it before."

"Let's call this a refresher course."

She smiled. "I appreciate your help in getting some time with Maddy."

"I want this settled as soon as possible. I heard in town today some ugly rumors flying around about Byron challenging you as sheriff. Obviously he's come out vocally against your right to be sheriff."

She squeezed her hands into fists. "I don't think he

wants to be sheriff, but he does want to control the person who is."

"All the more reason to vote for you."

Ben's stamp of approval strangely eased her tension at the mention of the man trying to make her life difficult. "Thanks."

"Look, that's Maddy with Lynne and Christie. Their FFA meeting must be over with."

Lucy examined Ben's innocent expression, except for a mischievous gleam dancing in his eyes. "What a coincidence. When did you hear they were going to be here tonight?"

"Am I that obvious?"

"Actually it's quite sweet, but—"

"Our food is here," Ben interrupted her and removed his wallet. "I'm paying for this."

"Bribing the sheriff?"

"You're off duty."

"I'm always on duty. At least several times a month my sleep is disrupted because of a call I need to deal with. Some folks think only the sheriff should take care of their problem."

"Like Byron McKay."

She chuckled. "That's putting it mildly. He's at the top of the list."

"My sleep was disrupted last night. Cody is getting a tooth and was not a happy camper. He didn't want anyone else sleeping since he wasn't."

"What did you do?"

"Rubbed a numbing gel on the area, then rocked him until he fell asleep. We moved him upstairs to give Grandma a break and me experience taking care of him.

I'm learning all kinds of stuff from Mamie and Chloe. I'm gonna be an expert by the time he's eighteen."

"That sounds as though you're preparing for more children." She'd never thought of Ben as a father. He never stayed with a woman long enough.

"I'm not opposed to the idea. Cody is quickly becoming the center of my life."

If she hadn't seen him with his son the other day, she wouldn't have believed a word he said. This change in Ben had taken her by surprise, but it shouldn't have if she considered his interest in young people and the intern program.

"I already know what not to do."

"You do?"

"Let just say the last years with my dad were a good lesson in what not to do. He barely tolerated me. He'd have kicked me off the ranch if Grady hadn't left to serve his country. He figured I was better than nothing."

"How are you and Grady getting along?" They were opposites. Grady had always been the serious one, disciplined and in control.

"I'm glad he came back. The ranch needed him."

"But not you?"

"When he left the last time he came home, I was glad he was gone. He was always on my case. This time is different. For one, it's time we become brothers in the true sense of the word. We weren't always at such odds. When we were younger, we got along."

"What happened?"

Ben shrugged. "We grew apart. My interests became different."

"Girls?"

"Not totally." He cocked his head to the side. "I think

it really began when my father seemed to favor Grady over me. If we were working on a project, he got the compliment. I was an afterthought."

She glimpsed the waitress bringing their tray of food. After Lucy passed Ben his dinner, he leaned over and handed the young girl the money to pay. His arm brushed against hers, and his scent, not unpleasant but outdoorsy, swirled around her.

When the waitress left and he sat back, Lucy realized she'd been holding her breath and finally exhaled. "I'm glad you and Grady are getting reacquainted. He hated seeing you like that in the hospital." And so had she. For a while she'd wondered if he would ever recover consciousness, and the thought of not seeing Ben's teasing smile again had bothered her more than she realized. "What are you going to do when Chloe has her baby?"

"That's a good question. At the very least I need a nanny. I won't leave Cody for Mamie to handle all the time by herself. Don't tell her that. She would protest. But what Cody really needs is a mother."

"You, settle down with one woman?"

"That's not an impossibility if I find the right person."

"What are you looking for?"

"Someone who loves children, has a good sense of humor, knows what she wants and…"

She waited half a minute before saying, "And what?"

"There is a connection between us—chemistry. Any suggestions on how to find a mother for Cody?"

In that moment, his gaze locked with hers, robbing her of any response. A lump swelled into her throat, taking her by surprise. She wanted the best for Cody—and Ben. "Let me think on it. Cody is a special kid. You'll only want the best for him."

His eyes gleamed. "Of course. He's a Stillwater." He took a long sip of his milk shake, watching her the whole time.

Goose bumps ran up her arms, and she focused on eating her juicy hamburger, savoring its delicious taste while ignoring the man so close to her in the sheriff's SUV.

"Looks as if the girls are leaving," Ben said while returning Maddy's wave.

"If she didn't know we were here before, she does now."

"Let them think what they want, especially if it helps you with solving the robberies."

"I'm going to check around about the music box and the necklace. They look expensive, so I might be able to find where they were bought."

"Not if they were bought online."

Lucy peered at Ben. "You think like a police officer. True, but it's worth looking into."

"While you do that, I can look on the internet and see if I can find a place that sells either one."

"I should do that."

"I want to help. Anything to get Byron off his high horse. It's okay to ask for help, and remember, I'm now part of the Rustling Investigation Team."

"As if you don't have enough to do."

"I could say the same thing to you."

She nodded once. "Touché." After washing down her last bite of food with the iced tea, Lucy balled the wrapping paper and stuffed it into the sack. "Ready. I'm one short at the station, so I imagine tomorrow will be busy."

"I understand you're going to be the maid of honor for Chloe."

Lucy grinned. "I'm so happy for her. She deserves a good man after that husband she had. I can't believe a guy leaving because his wife was pregnant with his child."

"Seeing her with Cody, I can tell Chloe is going to be a great mother."

She needed to find someone like Chloe for Ben. In the next few days she would take a look at the single females in Little Horn. If not, in the towns nearby.

"Will Eva and Tyler be back for the wedding?" Lucy turned onto the highway heading out of town.

"Yes, the day before."

"Good. Eva was rooting for Grady and Chloe."

"There seem to be a lot of happy couples recently."

"Yeah," she murmured, wondering if Jesse and she had worked out in San Antonio where she would be today. She liked her life in Little Horn, in spite of Byron being on her case, and was glad she discovered Jesse's tendency to be unfaithful. Never again. One Don Juan in her life was enough.

Suddenly a movement up ahead caught her attention, and she straightened, leaning forward to see better. "What are they doing?"

In her headlights, two figures, dressed in dark hoodies, were illuminated on the side of the road, holding up something between them. They froze for a few seconds in the bright glare, then dropped the sign, whirled around and raced into the field beside the road.

As she came to a stop on the shoulder where the two people had been, she reached for her flashlight. "Was that the town sign they were holding?"

Chapter Five

"It looked like it." Ben gripped the handle of Lucy's sheriff's SUV, ready to get out.

"Those two are long gone by now, but I want to check the area out." After she retrieved her weapon from the glove compartment, practically leaning across Ben, she climbed from the car and strapped on her gun belt.

Trying to ignore the jump in his pulse rate created by her nearness, Ben exited the car and started for where the two people had been. "I'm coming with you." She was the one wearing the firearm, not him, but something deep inside him wouldn't let him sit in the car and wait for her to investigate. What if the guys were watching from the brush? What if they tried to harm her? He wouldn't let that happen.

"If it would do any good, I'd tell you to wait in the car." Lucy went through the overgrown grass and weeds, coming to a stop a few feet in front of Ben. She shone her flashlight at the ground. "This is the sign stolen months ago."

Ben skirted her and bent over to pick up the metal plaque proclaiming, Welcome to Little Horn, Texas.

"Don't. Leave it. I want to run fingerprints on the sign."

"Now?" Ben straightened and faced her.

"No. I'll be right back." Lucy trudged to her vehicle and opened the rear hatch, then the back doors. A half a minute later she returned and handed him a pair of latex gloves. "I need your help carrying the sign to my SUV. I put the backseat down so we can get this inside."

"Sure." He snapped on the gloves and lifted one end while being careful not to touch any more of the sign than was necessary to carry it. "Everything happened so quickly, but it looked as though the two guys had on gloves."

"They did. I'm hoping they haven't been that careful in the past."

Ben stopped at one side of the rear bumper. "Won't there be tons of prints on the sign?"

"I know this is a long shot, but I can't ignore this piece of evidence. The new welcome sign has been up for several years, and I've doubt many have touched it since the initial installation."

After they slid the piece of evidence into the back, Lucy shut the rear hatch and started back to the area.

"What are you doing?" Ben followed her.

"I'm going to check the ground for any evidence in case one of them left something behind. Once they left a watch at a crime scene and one came back to get it. We almost had him, but he got away. My life would be much easier if I had."

"I wonder why they brought it back." Ben stood back from the area while Lucy shone her light on the tramped grass.

"This is one of the reasons I think the Robin Hoods

are teenagers. Anyone interested in making money by stealing cattle and equipment wouldn't have bothered taking the sign. But these robbers are making a statement. They are angry."

"Then, why return the sign?"

Lucy took one last look, then joined Ben at the edge. "I don't think their anger is directed at the whole town, and this sign belongs to everyone. I think they've finally realized that."

"It makes sense. Hopefully they realize stealing is wrong and want to make amends." Ben walked beside her to the car. "I'll keep an ear out with the girls at the ranch. You can't always be there when they are, but I can try to be. I might be able to overhear something." Reaching around her, he grasped the driver's-side door and opened it for her.

"The day I can bring these guys in can't come fast enough for me." She slid behind the steering wheel.

"We'll have to celebrate when that day comes." Ben leaned down, her fresh, clean scent wafting to him. In the dim interior light, her crystalline green eyes transfixed him and held him rooted to the spot.

"I'd like that." A smile transformed her mouth from a thoughtful look to a radiant one.

She was beautiful, but even more than that he liked her caring and integrity. He pulled back and shut the door, then rounded the cruiser to sit on his side.

As she drove through the gates of the Stillwater Ranch, Ben relaxed back against the seat. "I hope you'll come in. Mamie usually has a pot of decaf coffee on at this time. She makes the best coffee."

"I know. I've had it before. Do you think Chloe will be there? I'd like to talk to her about the wedding next week. I want to make sure I do everything I need to as a maid of honor. This is my first time being one."

"She should be. I wonder if I need to throw Grady a bachelor party."

"I get the impression they want it low-key, but it's a good question to ask them." Lucy pulled up in front of the large, sprawling white Western-style Colonial house. "I've always thought your home fit your ranch, whereas Byron's flashy mansion doesn't really fit in Little Horn."

"Byron does everything with grandeur."

"Even when he's a pain."

Laughing, Ben unlocked the front door and stepped to the side to allow Lucy to enter first. In the foyer, he poked his head into the living room, saw Grandma reading her Bible and waited until she glanced up. "Where's Cody?"

"Asleep."

"That's early."

"He didn't nap well again today, so he was tired earlier than usual." His grandmother closed her Bible and put it on the end table next to her on the couch, smiling when Lucy came into view. "It's good to see you again. How did the meeting go?"

Lucy stopped beside Ben. "With no new robberies, we went over what's being done to find the Robin Hoods. But on the way here, we," she said with a pause, slanting a look at Ben, "saw two guys trying to put the town's welcome sign back in place."

Mamie's eyes grew round. "You caught the Robin Hoods?"

Lucy shook her head. "But I have the sign and will put it back up tomorrow."

"Good." Mamie pushed to her feet, her shoulders sagging as though she was fatigued. "There's fresh coffee in the kitchen. I'm going to follow Cody to bed early tonight."

"Grandma, where are Grady and Chloe?"

She walked toward the hallway, paused and turned toward them. "Out on the back porch, discussing their wedding plans. Good night, y'all." Then she continued toward her downstairs bedroom in the back.

Ben watched her and wanted to help her, but when he had tried a few days ago to talk to her about slowing down, she'd lashed into him, informing him she was just fine. He leaned toward Lucy's ear. "I want her to do less, but she refuses."

"That sounds like her. She told me she is as young as she thinks she is."

"Let's get coffee, then go out back." He took her hand and tugged her toward the kitchen. When she didn't move, he glanced back at Lucy.

She stared at their clasped hands, then up at him, her forehead creased, her green eyes dark.

"We're friends, Lucy. That's all." He released his grasp and pivoted toward the hallway that led to the kitchen. It was clear that was all Lucy wanted, and that bothered him.

Lucy sat in a comfortable, cushioned chair on the back porch at Stillwater Ranch and listened to Grady and Ben talking about pranks they pulled on each other growing up. Laughter surrounded her, and she even joined in, but she couldn't shake the sensations that had flooded her when Ben had taken her hand in the hallway.

For a split second, a connection had sprung up between them that had nothing to do with being friends.

It had come out of nowhere, and she didn't know why. She'd known Ben all of her life and had seen him often except for those years she'd spent in San Antonio. Was he really different since he'd woken up from the coma?

Chloe turned to Lucy and said in a low voice, "These past weeks, it's as if Ben and Grady are reacquainting themselves."

"As teens they became more adversaries than brothers. I'm glad to see them like this."

"Maybe it takes near-death experiences for a person to see what's important."

Lucy slanted a glance at the brothers. "Who are you talking about, Ben or Grady?"

"Both, in a way. The war changed Grady."

"What are y'all whispering about over there?" Ben asked in a teasing voice.

"Our own childhood escapades. You two aren't the only ones. Chloe and I were friends growing up."

Ben chuckled and looked at his twin brother. "I believe we've been ignoring the womenfolk."

"Womenfolk!" Chloe burst out laughing.

Again Lucy responded to the humor in Ben's expression. When they were growing up, he'd often thrown caution to the wind and dived into something he wanted to do without considering the risks. Sometimes she wished she had that ability. "Yes, you have been ignoring us. I can't stay long. I have an early day tomorrow. This conversation is supposed to be about the wedding. I know, Chloe, you told me not to worry. Just show up at the church Friday afternoon. But surely I can do something for you and Grady."

Chloe shook her head. "There isn't any time. We did it this way because we didn't want a fuss made."

"How about I have a luncheon for you on Thursday at my house? A few friends. Nothing fancy, since I'll be making it." Lucy took a sip of her coffee.

"Well, in that case, Grady, we should have a little gathering with a few friends," Ben chimed in. "I can't let Lucy outdo me in the department of maid of honor/best man."

"This isn't a contest, Ben." Lucy set her empty mug on the table nearby.

"The dinner here after the wedding is all we want." Grady said as he and Chloe both stood at the same time. He took Chloe's hand. "It's been a long day for Chloe. I'm gonna escort her to her bedroom, then check with Zed at the barn about the cattle rotation."

Chloe nodded. "If you want to do something, I'll let you give me a baby shower closer to the due date. Okay, Lucy?"

"Short of hog-tying you and kidnapping you to come to the luncheon, I have to accept your wishes." Lucy grinned. "Mainly I want you to know I'm here if you need me. Just ask."

As Grady slung his arm over Chloe's shoulder and started for the back door, his fiancée replied, "I will."

When they disappeared into the house, Lucy remembered the glow of love on her friend's face. Chloe stayed at the ranch because of Cody and slept in her own room connected to the baby's. Lucy wished she could find a love like Chloe and Grady had, but she couldn't seem to get past Jesse's betrayal. She wasn't the risk taker Ben was.

"We could always throw a surprise party for each of them. For it to work we would have to do it at the same time." Ben slouched back in his chair, his elbows on the arms and his hands clasped in front of him.

"And lose my best friend? No way."

"Yeah, Grady wouldn't be too happy with me, either. We're starting to work out our past differences. That might add fuel to the fire."

"It was nice hearing you all talk about the good times."

"It's been a long while since we did."

"It's time to put the past where it belongs. In the past."

A twinkle in his dark brown eyes followed with a half grin preceded him saying, "In your infinite wisdom, you're correct."

"All I ask is for you to remember just what you said when you start to argue with me." She rose. "I need to leave. Finding the town sign adds another task to my long list for tomorrow."

"Let me know when you're going to put it back up. I think the area around it needs to be tended. That would be a good task for my three interns. Of course, I'd want your input in how to do it. Maybe you can help or supervise us."

"Ben Stillwater, you are a good man to have on a team. I appreciate the offer and accept. I was thinking about it when tramping through the tall grass and weeds this evening. If we let it go too long, then no one will be able to see the sign."

"I could give you the cliché line about brilliant minds thinking alike, but I won't. I was thinking if Maddy is the reason our ranch hasn't been hit, then having her work on the sign-beautification project might keep it safe this time." He stood, grabbing his mug, then reaching for hers…at the same time she did.

Their fingers touched. Their gazes embraced. All thoughts fled Lucy's mind. A lock of his sandy-brown hair fell over one eye. The urge to brush it back inundated her and sobered her to the effect he had on her. She had to find him someone who would be a good wife and mother. Then everything would get back to normal between them. It was clearly not going to be her, a tomboyish, work-dedicated sheriff.

She snatched the mug and brought it up to her chest as though it was a barrier between them. "I'd better go."

She marched toward the back door and hurried inside, needing to put some space between them. Fast. She'd promised herself as a teenager she would never fall for his charm. She'd seen him break one girl's heart after another. Not hers.

After putting the mug in the sink, she pivoted to head into the hallway and ran right into Ben.

He stepped back—thankfully—and set his cup next to hers. "I'll walk you to your car."

"You don't need to. Remember you're recovering from a serious accident."

"Please, don't remind me. I'm trying to put that incident in my past." One corner of his mouth quirked.

"Good. I'm glad you're learning how." She sidestepped him and strode toward the hallway. Now if only she could learn to put her past behind her. She hated the idea that Jesse's betrayal still affected her. But it did.

He moved ahead of her and opened the front door.

As she passed him, she said, "I'm going to have to compliment Mamie on raising such a gentleman."

His chuckles filled the night air and sent ripples of awareness of the man walking beside her to her car. Again he opened her driver's-side door.

"You know, a gal could get used to this," she said as she slipped into her sheriff's SUV, rolling down her window. "Good night, and thanks for coming up with ways for me to get closer to Maddy."

He leaned against the car, his elbows on the open window. "You're welcome. Anything to help a friend."

When she started the engine, he pushed back and stayed there as she drove away. She took one last glimpse of him as she drove around the curve toward the main gates of the ranch.

The whole way to town, her mind raced with possible women for him to date. What about Ingrid Edwards? She was husband hunting, declaring she wanted to be married by twenty-six, which wasn't too far away. No, she was too needy. Jenna Thorn might be a possibility. Ben knew her because she was Carson's sister. No, she didn't have her life together.

By the time she reached her small house in Little Horn, her thoughts swirled with eligible women in the area. She let herself in and put her purse on the counter in the kitchen, decorated in tones of green and burgundy—her mom's touches. When her parents left to travel throughout the United States, she'd moved into her childhood home and she still hadn't made any changes to it. One day she hoped they'd be returning to Little Horn. Then she would find her own place to live.

Suddenly a name popped into her head for Ben: Paula Morris, the only Realtor in town. She would be a good candidate for Ben. She was pretty, sensible and nice. Perfect.

Lucy rode on Daisy Mae, a pinto mare, beside Ben the next day across the pasture near the barn. "I met with

Paula Morris today about looking for a place for me to live in the area, hopefully in Little Horn."

"Are your parents coming back to town to live?" Ben slowed his stallion to a walk.

"They haven't said anything, but every time I talk to Mom, it sounds as though she misses home. I've been saving up to buy my own place for the day they do return for longer than a visit." Lucy slid a glance at Ben. "Paula knows this area inside and out. There isn't anything right now, but she'll let me know when something does come up."

"You're thinking of moving to another town in the county?"

"I might have to. Of course, if I don't get reelected, I might have to look for another job, too."

Ben's jawline hardened. "I'm not gonna let Byron get his way. You'll be reelected."

"You want to be head of my reelection campaign?"

"Me?" He stopped Thunder and looked at her. "Are you kidding?"

She brought Daisy Mae to a halt and twisted around so she faced Ben. "You know this county well, and whenever you do something you go all out. I couldn't ask for a better campaign manager."

He tipped his black Stetson. "Well, thank you, ma'am. I just might do it, but it's not for another year. I try not to plan too far in the future. I've learned it can change in a blink of an eye."

"True. Speaking of Paula, you two would make a nice couple."

One of his eyebrows rose beneath his hat. "When were we speaking of Paula and dating? You mentioned looking for a place to live." His mouth pinched together. "Or was that a way to bring up Paula?"

"Yes. I've been giving it a lot of thought since you talked about finding a nanny or wife soon. You've been out of circulation for months. Paula wouldn't be the nanny, but she isn't dating anyone now. She's pretty..."

Ben urged his stallion into a gallop, leaving Lucy to watch his back. Obviously Paula didn't fit his idea of a date. Okay. She would come up with someone else.

She nudged her mare into a gallop and arrived at the barn a couple of minutes behind Ben.

He'd handed his reins to Christie to take care of Thunder while he said to Maddy, "Show Lucy how to care for her mount when she comes back from a hard ride."

"Will do." Maddy waited by Daisy Mae while Lucy dismounted, then the teenage girl handed Lucy the reins. "We'll do what we did earlier in reverse." She ran her hand over the mare's neck. "She's sweating, so we'll cool her off after that."

"She's a good horse for me. She seems to know what she needs to do with little prompting from me. Do you ride much, Maddy?"

"I have since I started working here. Ben lets us ride several times a week. He said that's part of learning ranching—becoming an extension of your horse. That's my favorite part of the job." Maddy removed the saddle and the blanket under it and put them on a rack.

"I see you're wearing the necklace your secret admirer gave you. Do you know who he is?"

Maddy blushed. "No."

"Who would you like it to be?"

Christie walked by with Thunder and said, "Gareth McKay, if she was smart."

"Christie!" Maddy's cheeks reddened even more.

"You know he has a serious crush on you. All you'd have to do is show him you're interested and he'd ask you out."

Maddy took the reins from Lucy. "Ignore her. She doesn't know anything. Gareth would never be interested in me."

"Why?"

"He's the son of the wealthiest man in the county. I know his father would never allow it. Gareth's father wouldn't even have anything to do with Betsy, his cousin."

"Ah, so you like Gareth."

The teenager turned away, her shoulders slumped. "I'll take it from here. All we're gonna do is walk the horses until they are cooled down, then I'll turn Daisy Mae out in the pasture."

Lucy caught up with her walking toward the rear door. "Maddy, you have a lot to offer a person. You're a hard worker, and according to Ben, you're a natural with the animals."

"But I'm in foster care. I have no family." Her eyes widened. "Don't get me wrong. My foster parents are good to me, but when I become eighteen and graduate from high school, I'm on my own."

"What do you want to do?"

"Ultimately I want to be a vet and work with big animals, but the money..." Maddy cleared her throat. "Since I can't do that, training horses would be a good job.".

"You've got another year. There are loans and scholarships out there you might be able to apply for."

Her eyes glistening, Maddy looked at her. "My grades

are all right, As and Bs, but the competition for those scholarships is stiff."

Lucy gave Maddy a hug. "Keep doing the kind of work you do here, and you'll have people to champion your cause."

Maddy pulled back, swiping at a tear that rolled down her cheek. "I try not to think about the future, but sometimes I do and I always get discouraged. For several years I've known this is what I'm supposed to do with my life."

"God has a plan for you. He'll provide a way." Lucy's throat thickened. The young girl touched her heart. If she could help Maddy, she would.

"I know. That's what Pastor Mathers says. I reckon he knows what he's talking about."

"A wise man. I'll see you at dinner."

Maddy continued her trek toward the rear of the barn. Lucy watched the girl, her shoulders squaring, her head held up.

"What were y'all talking about?" Ben whispered behind her.

She jerked, surprised by his presence. She'd been so wrapped up in Maddy she hadn't realized he was nearby. "She wants to be a vet and doesn't see how she'll be able to do that."

"When the time comes, the Lone Star Cowboy League might be able to help her like they did for Tyler when he wanted to be a doctor. We've been talking about doing it on a regular basis for a youth around here who can't afford college otherwise."

A smile spread through her. "Right. That's one possibility. She certainly has the need and she's a good kid."

"Did she say anything to help your case?"

"She likes Gareth. Not sure if he returns the feelings or not, but I'm going to check around. Gareth McKay has the money to buy those gifts for Maddy, and he has a tie to Betsy."

"Let's go to the house. The girls know to come up to the house a little before six." He ambled toward the front entrance. "Are you thinking the Robin Hoods are Gareth and his twin, Winston?"

She glanced at her watch, surprised to see it was five forty already. When she was with Ben, time seemed to race by. "They fit the body type we saw last night, they know about ranches and cattle and have access to equipment to move the cattle."

"You'll need more than speculation before you confront Byron and his sons."

"I know, and I could be wrong. The twins are connected to Betsy, and now Gareth with Maddy. I should hear from the New Mexico State Police about the man they caught moving stolen cattle near the Texas border. And I'm still making inquiries about the music box and necklace. So far nothing in the immediate area. Did you find anything online?"

"No, but there are tons of places on the internet that would sell something like that. I doubt I'll find half of them."

"I know it's a long shot, but that's how some cases are solved. A lot of legwork, or in your case, finger work."

"How are you doing with the physical places?"

"In this county, I'm visiting the stores and taking a picture of the items to see if they sell them."

"What if it's somewhere like Austin or even San Antonio?" Ben placed his hand at the small of her back as they mounted the stairs to the front porch.

"I'm going to fax the picture and inquiry. My dispatcher/receptionist is making a list of ones in the Austin area for me. I'm hoping it doesn't go that far away, though." The feel of his light touch zipped up her spine and reminded her of when he took her hand last night. She hadn't expected it and had been surprised by it.

"Then you have Fort Worth and Dallas north of us."

She moaned. "Don't remind me. This is the drudgery part of being a police officer."

"Not stakeouts?" He opened the front door.

"With a stakeout there's the anticipation you'll discover something important to crack your case."

In the hallway he faced her. "You really enjoy what you do."

Although not a question, she nodded. "Ever since I went to work with Dad one day when I was twelve, I've wanted to be a police officer. You never know what to expect."

"I can see the enthusiasm on your face when you talk about your job. That's the way I feel about running this ranch."

"You used to accuse me of being an open book. I probably would never be good at undercover work." The sounds of giggles coming from the living room drew her attention.

"That's Cody. In a short time I've learned his laughter and can tell what a few of his cries mean. Well, Grandma helped me with that one." Ben swept his arm toward the living room.

When he entered behind Lucy, Cody saw him and began crawling to him. Ben met him halfway, scooped up his son and swung him around. The baby's laughter echoed through the room. "This has become our routine when I see him." Ben stopped turning and held his son.

Lucy looked around the pair and said, "It's nice to see you, Mamie." She took in a deep breath of the aroma floating from the kitchen. "Thanks for the dinner invitation. It smells wonderful."

The older woman rose slowly. "Now that y'all are here to watch Cody, I'm going to help Martha Rose set the table and put the food on."

"Can I help, too?"

"No, you're a guest. Enjoy Cody."

After Mamie left, his son's small hand reached up and grabbed the brim of Ben's cowboy hat, then yanked on it. The Stetson tumbled off his head with a little encouragement from him. It hit the floor between Ben and Lucy.

He put Cody down by the black hat. "Watch this," he said and stepped back by Lucy.

Cody sat up next to it and dragged the Stetson to him. He lifted it but couldn't get his head under it. Finally Ben plopped it on his son's head and tilted it back so Cody could see out the front.

"I'm definitely getting you a hat, little man, and then cowboy boots when you start walking." He ruffled his son's dark hair and took his Stetson to hang on the peg in the hallway.

Lucy knelt near Cody, seeing his face screwing up for a protest. She swept him into her arms and stood. "Look at all the toys you have." She moved to a few scattered ones on the floor in front of the coffee table. "I haven't stacked rings in a *long* time. Can you show me how?" She handed him the red doughnut-shaped toy.

It went into Cody's mouth, and he gnawed on it.

Ben squatted next to Lucy. "He's teething and loves

to chew on anything he can get into his mouth. I used to let him have my hat longer until he began trying to eat the brim."

While Ben interacted with his son, Lucy sat cross-legged next to them and enjoyed the scene. Ben was good with Cody, as if he instinctively knew what to do. He hadn't been involved in his child's life for long, but a person wouldn't know it. He was born to be a father, in spite of the strained relationship with his own dad.

When Ben lay on the floor and Cody crawled onto his chest, Lucy marveled at the sight. Ben had told her he was a changed man. Maybe he was after all.

Chapter Six

The sound of cries penetrated Ben's sleep, yanking him awake. He sat up straight, his heartbeat kicking up a notch. Cody was awake.

Ben slipped out of bed, glancing at the clock on the bedside table. Four in the morning. The cries increased, and he hurried his pace to Cody's bedroom down the hall. When he came into his room, his son stood up in his crib, his face beet red as he worked himself into a rage.

Ben shut the door and rushed to pick up Cody. "Shh. I'm here. You'll be okay."

He sat in the rocking chair and started going back and forth. His son's screams blasted his ears. Ben checked to see if Cody was wet. No. He shouldn't be hungry yet. It must be his teeth. After he applied the numbing gel in the area where a tooth was coming in, he rocked his son, humming a lullaby Grandma Mamie used sometimes.

In the dim glow of the night-light, Cody's eyes began to slide close, only to snap open, then do it all over again. "Shh. Don't fight it, son," Ben said in a singsong voice.

As his child fell asleep, Ben leaned back and closed his eyes, relishing the soft bundle in his arms. Love and a fierce protective instinct assailed him. If he'd known this was what being a father felt like, he would have seriously considered settling down years ago. Looking back over his life, he realized his behavior had started because his own father had criticized everything he did. His rebellion had become a contest between them. He didn't want that for Cody and him.

Lord, I know I haven't been the best son to You or my father. Show me what I need to do to make this right. I want to have the kind of relationship Lucy has with her dad.

He could remember seeing Lucy as a deputy sheriff working for her father. They had been a team. He couldn't recall his dad and him ever having been like that.

When Cody was sound asleep, Ben slowly rose and placed him gently in the crib. He kissed the tips of two fingers and lightly touched his son's cheek. His heart swelled at the sight of Cody at peace and content. He wished he was. His life was unsettled—had been for years, if he was truthful with himself.

After leaving his son's room, Ben headed downstairs. It was after five. No sense trying to go back to sleep. He was usually up by six or six thirty anyway. In the kitchen, he made a pot of coffee that could tide him over until his grandmother got up. His brew wasn't nearly as good as hers.

As it perked, he lounged against the counter, his legs crossed and arms folded. He stared at the tile floor. A lot had happened in town but also here at the ranch. He still wanted to go forward with a summer camp for kids—for Cody. If he started small this summer, he could expand in the years to follow if it worked.

"What great world affairs are you contemplating?" Grady asked from the doorway.

Ben glanced at him. "A summer camp. We have that old barn we could use with some renovations."

"For who?"

"Kids."

Grady laughed. "I kinda figured that one out."

Ben pushed off the counter and crossed to the coffeepot. "Want some?"

"Sure."

While Ben filled two mugs, he said, "I'm still trying to figure it all out. I started last fall in hopes of having something for this summer. Since my accident delayed that, I thought about having one week this year, maybe in conjunction with the church. If it went well, then I would expand it for the following year."

"That's a mighty tall order."

"When I first got home from the hospital, I kept thinking I could pull it off for this summer. Have the camp in June and July." Ben cocked a grin. "Since then common sense has taken hold. I can't do it all in that short amount of time, especially the way I want it to be, but one week is doable and a good start to see how it would go."

"One week would still be a lot of extra work."

"I can do it, especially if you're back to stay. It would allow me more time to devote to planning the summer camp."

Grady sat at the table, his eyebrows slashing down. "I never figured you for something like this."

"Why, because I was a woman-chasing man?"

"Frankly, yes." Grady took a drink of his coffee.

"That's not me anymore. I have Cody to think of. If

you're not staying, I'll do it anyway. It will start on a small scale. The children can learn everything about the ranch. The intern program through the school would be a great place to hire counselors. Our place is doing well, and I want to give back some."

"Is this a free camp?"

Grady had always been the practical one growing up, and Ben had learned that necessity as he ran the ranch, but he still liked to dream. "Not exactly, but there would be a sliding scale depending on the parents' ability to pay. So, yes, there would be some that would attend free." As he talked about his vision to help the community, excitement built in him. His accident might have delayed the project, but it didn't mean he had to abandon it.

"Who else knows about this?"

"Grandma, Lucy and Carson. I actually got the idea from one of the interns in the high school program. The teen grew up in town and hadn't been exposed to a lot of ranch life earlier. Carson said he would be interested in the Lone Star Cowboy League being a part of it." Ben sipped his coffee, studying his brother's expression. He should know him better, but for years he'd served in the army and been gone. Grady's experience in the war zone had affected him, even changed him, but Ben realized one incident could do that. They had that in common.

A slow grin spread across his twin's face. "I like it."

Ben relaxed back against the chair. "Good. I'm going to talk with Pastor Mathers and see if we can hold the Vacation Bible School here this summer as a start. After that, I'll know how to proceed forward, but I'm glad I have your backing."

"And help."

Those two words meant a lot to Ben. He hoped that he and his brother could mend their relationship. This could be a start.

On Sunday before and during the service at Little Horn Community Christian Church, Lucy had scanned the young women, trying to come up with another candidate for Ben either as a nanny or a possible wife. Her gaze fell on Abigail Bardera, who worked at Maggie's Coffee Shop as a waitress. She was friendly, polite even to demanding customers like Byron; she was also attractive and not dating anyone.

As the crowd filed out of the pews, Lucy stood and made her way toward the exit. Now all she had to figure out was how to casually bring up Abigail to Ben, at least better than when she did Paula.

"Your problem can't be that bad," Ben whispered behind her.

She glanced over her shoulder. "Where did you come from?"

"From the front pew where Mamie wanted to sit."

"Oh, I thought you had already left."

"I had, but Mamie had left her Bible in the pew and I came back to pick it up." He stepped beside her, holding up the black book.

As they shuffled forward in the line waiting to shake hands with Pastor Mathers, Lucy asked, "Where's Cody?"

"In the nursery. How would you like to have a picnic with Cody and me? I wanted to start showing my son the ranch."

"I don't know. I…" She couldn't think of a reason

not to, and it would be nice to take some time off from thinking about the Robin Hoods.

"Are you working today?"

"No—well, sort of. I have laundry to do and some chores around the house."

"Surely you'd rather go riding with Cody and me."

She fastened her gaze onto his dimples. When he turned them on her, it was hard to resist him. "Actually, anything would be better than housework."

He chuckled. "I'm not sure if that was an insult or not."

She grinned. "It wasn't meant to be. When are you going?"

"When I get home. I can have Martha Rose make us something for lunch. We can have a picnic. The weather is great. We should be outside on a day like this. You've been working too hard. You need to play some, too."

"I thought you said you were changing."

"I am, but I'll always relax and take time to enjoy life. Even the Lord took a day of rest. You're much too serious."

"And you aren't," she said without thinking. She wanted to take those words back because she had seen a change in Ben. But would it last?

"I have my moments," Ben whispered into her ear.

She slowly moved forward, thinking way too much about Ben's breath tickling her neck. When it was her turn to talk to Pastor Mathers, for a few seconds her mind went blank.

The pastor shook her hand, yanking her out of her fixation on Ben beside her. "I enjoyed your sermon today on forgiveness."

"I just hope some members of the congregation were

listening with all that has been going on these past six months."

"Emotions have been running high. When we find the Robin Hoods, I wouldn't want to be in their shoes. Good day." Lucy moved forward and paused to wait for Ben.

"I need to see you this week about Vacation Bible School this summer. I have a proposition for you," Ben said after greeting the pastor.

"Why don't we talk before or after the meeting with the Easter-egg hunt committee?" Pastor Mathers looked at Lucy. "We are still meeting Tuesday night at the church, aren't we?"

"Yes, most of the planning has been done, but we still have a few items to discuss."

"Good. Ben, I'll talk to you then. The meeting is at six. Is five thirty okay?"

"That's fine with me. I can't believe Easter is only weeks away." Ben nodded his head at the pastor, then joined Lucy.

"I need to go home and change. I'll meet you at the ranch in half an hour. Is that okay?"

"I'll be at the barn." He headed for the nursery.

As Lucy started for her car, she nearly collided with Byron. She glanced away to see where his sons and wife were. They weren't around. "Excuse me."

Byron moved into her path. "How's the investigation going?"

"We're following some promising leads. You'll be one of the first to know when we catch the robbers."

"How come your friend, Ben, hasn't been hit? Have you ever asked yourself that? Maybe it's one of his hired hands or..." Snapping his mouth closed, Byron peered beyond Lucy.

"I couldn't help but overhear your question to the sheriff." Ben held his son in his arms. "You'll have to ask the Robin Hoods when they're found." He handed Cody to Lucy, then crowded into Byron's personal space. "Don't you start accusing anyone connected with the Stillwater Ranch. I won't take it like others have."

The bluster in Byron faded, but his face reddened as he looked around at the people nearby. "It's a question we need to ask of anyone who hasn't been hit by the robbers."

"A better question is why were you hit a number of times. I believe from what I've heard since I woke up from my coma, you've been a victim of the Robin Hoods more than anyone else. Why? What makes you so special?"

Byron glared at Ben, opened his mouth but only ended up snorting before he stepped around Ben and hurried toward the meeting hall.

Lucy panned the faces of the congregation around them. Smiles graced the people's expressions.

Tom Horton came forward and clapped Ben on the shoulder. "Welcome back. We've missed your candor."

To the side and behind Ben stood the twins, Winston and Gareth, gaping at the scene. Lucy peered over her shoulder to see if Byron was around. He wasn't.

She started for the teenage boys but behind her, Byron called, "Winston. Gareth. Your mother is wondering where you are."

The twins plodded toward their father in the doorway into the meeting hall.

She sighed.

Ben appeared in front of her. "Sorry about that. I

couldn't let him start in on you at church or on anyone working at my ranch."

"I can take care of myself, but thanks for thinking of me. I'll see you in half an hour."

As Lucy drove home to change into jeans and a T-shirt, her hands gripped the steering wheel so tight they ached. In her driveway, she released her tight grasp and wiggled her fingers. Byron was like a burr under a saddle blanket. When she approached him about interviewing his two sons, she had to have enough evidence to make a case against them or he would make her life miserable until time for reelection. It would be a *long* year for her.

It took ten minutes to change her clothes and jump into her Mustang to head to the Stillwater Ranch. She arrived a few moments ahead of schedule and decided to park at the house until she glimpsed Ben exiting the barn with Cody in his arms. When Ben waved, Lucy put her Mustang in Reverse and headed to the barn.

He opened the door to her vehicle with a big grin on his face. "That's what I love about you, Lucy Benson. You don't keep a man waiting. You're always on time—or before."

She climbed from her car, saw Cody's smile directed at her and held her arms out for the baby. "Cody, I wouldn't dare be late to meet you. Now, your daddy, on the other hand, is a whole different story."

"Waiting for you isn't a big chore," Ben said, then winked and walked toward the barn.

She trailed behind him. "That's because you don't have to. Remember what you said."

At the entrance, he swept around and plucked Cody

from her arms. "I'll let you saddle your horse first, then you can hold him while I take care of Thunder."

"What! You aren't going to do both?"

The dimples in his cheeks deepened. "Nope. I need to see if you learned anything from what Maddy showed you the other day."

She narrowed her eyes and proceeded to where he had Daisy Mae tied. Without a word she did everything correctly, even adjusting her stirrups to where they should be for her. Then she whirled about with her hand on her waist. "I'm not a total novice. I used to ride when I was younger. Remember? Here at your ranch?"

"Ah, yes. How could I forget those races you lost to me?"

She pursed her lips and marched to him, took Cody and kept going toward the rear exit. The baby played with her hair. When he stuck some strands in his mouth, she laughed and gently tugged them free.

"I'm glad my son can make you laugh. I need to take lessons from him."

"I won't be laughing if you put my hair in your mouth."

Forty-five minutes later, Ben laid Cody on the blanket, spread out under a large pine tree that blocked the sun. "I loved hearing his giggles as he rode with me. He's going to be a natural rider."

"Thunder was great letting him pat him over and over. I can't believe Cody fell asleep." Lucy settled next to the baby on one side while Ben did on the other.

"It's kinda like a rocking chair. He usually doesn't sleep for another hour, but he was up some last night because of his tooth coming in. I'll be glad when it's in."

"Then it'll start over with the next tooth."

"Please don't remind me." Ben lounged back, propping himself on his elbows.

"You'll do fine. From what I've seen, you've jumped in with both feet into this daddy gig."

"When I do something, that's the way I am. Why do it halfway?"

"All or nothing. Interesting."

Ben wasn't sure what she meant by that comment. Interesting how? But he held back asking Lucy. Since he'd woken up from his coma and left the hospital, his relationship with Lucy had shifted. He wasn't sure quite what was going on, but like riding a bronco, he was holding on tight and seeing where it was going. "Grady and I talked this morning. I told him about my summer camp I wanted to do, and he actually supported the idea. I think that is a first, at least in a long time."

"He was mighty worried about you while you were in the hospital. Just be careful. You've got a lot on your plate. Don't overload it."

"I've been out of the loop for months. All I did was sleep. I'm ready to tackle life again." Ben stared up at the pine needles above him, looking at a bright red cardinal on a branch. "I think the Lord gave me Cody for a reason."

"What reason?"

"I'm not sure yet. I was already planning a summer camp and getting involved in the intern program at the high school. When I pick up Cody, I feel at peace. I really never thought of myself as a father, especially with the bad relationship I had with my own. Grady seemed more likely to carry on the Stillwater name." Thoughts he'd been mulling over for weeks since he'd known about

Cody being a Stillwater came rushing out, surprising him. Why was he sharing this with Lucy?

"I never had any brothers or sisters. My parents were great, but I wanted siblings. They did, too, but Mom couldn't have any more children."

"I don't want Cody to be an only child. I know he'll have a cousin soon when Chloe gives birth, but it's not the same thing." Finally he looked at Lucy sitting cross-legged on the blanket facing him with a sleeping Cody in between. A blank expression hid her feelings. He wanted to know how she felt about having children, but ground his teeth to keep that question to himself.

She pushed herself to her feet. "I need to stretch my legs, especially after sitting in church, then on Daisy Mae."

"Not a bad idea. If I sit too much longer, I might go to sleep like Cody."

She gazed at his son. "It's always nice to see a baby sleeping so peacefully. Their only worries are when are they going to be fed and changed. Those were definitely simpler days, with no Byron around to bug me every day about the investigation."

"He is used to having things taken care of immediately when he wants something done."

"Believe me, I would if I could, but since I'm leaning more and more to Winston and Gareth, I need to have the evidence before I confront them. It would be nice if I didn't have to have Byron in the room when I interview them."

"Why would they rob their own ranch? To take any suspicion off them?"

"Maybe. I still think it's about Betsy. And if Gareth

is Maddy's secret admirer, can you imagine his father's reaction to that?"

Ben paused near the stream, turning to keep an eye on Cody still sleeping. "I remember Carson's father's reaction when he dated Ruby. His actions were what separated the two and made Ruby leave town. Thankfully they're together, but it took years before that happened. Like Ruby, Maddy is a good kid, and I think Gareth would be much better off dating her rather than some other girls."

"You're already starting to sound like a father. Remember that when Cody is Gareth's age."

Ben exaggerated a shiver. "I shudder to think about Cody being a teenager. Those days weren't that long ago for me. Looking back, I see where I didn't make it easy for my father and me to have a relationship. It wasn't all his fault. I couldn't have said that this time last year."

Lucy touched his arm. "A lot has happened to you since then."

"Yeah, like I missed part of it." He stepped closer, her fragrance mingling with the scents of nature surrounding them. "It's been good talking to you. I'm not there with Grady yet. As young boys, we were close. I'd like that back. I'm discovering how important home and family are."

"I miss my parents." She dropped her arm to her side.

He missed the connection. "Are they going to come back to Little Horn to stay one day?"

"I hope. We do have a close relationship, and conducting it long distance isn't the same thing as face-to-face."

He cocked a smile. "Even with video calling."

"Not even with that."

Inching forward, Ben clasped her shoulders. When

she didn't shrug away, he inhaled a deep breath of relief. There was something about Lucy that drew him. He wanted to explore these feelings, but Lucy only saw him as the man he used to be. "If you want, we can eat before Cody wakes up. I brought finger foods for him."

"What did Martha Rose fix for us?"

"Leftover fried chicken from yesterday, and as usual it was delicious. Some coleslaw and potato salad. Iced tea to drink."

"Sounds great," she murmured but didn't take a step toward the blanket.

And Ben was in no hurry to, either. "Your muscles are tight."

She nodded. "That's where my stress settles."

His gaze seized by hers, he kneaded her shoulders. He wanted to kiss her. He had for years, ever since she'd slapped him as a thirteen-year-old when he'd tried.

His hands stilled, then slipped to her face, framing it, her warm cheeks beneath his fingers, drawing him closer. Her mouth beckoned him. He slanted his head and slowly closed the distance between them and settled his lips over hers. The sensations bombarding him surprised him and yet didn't. He'd known kissing Lucy would be everything he dreamed as a teenager.

Cries pierced the air, shattering the brief moment.

Lucy pedaled backward, her eyes large, tiny lines grooving her forehead.

As much as he wanted to pursue what just happened between them, his son had awakened and didn't know where he was. He hurried toward Cody and scooped him up. "I'm right here, little man. I won't leave you."

Chapter Seven

With a sigh, Lucy eased into the chair at the head of the conference table at church. No one else had arrived yet for the meeting about the Easter-egg hunt, which was only ten days away. Today had been another long day, mostly spent between Bakersville and Blue Creek, towns on opposite sides of the county. One had been a good lead on an abandoned cattle trailer, but what she'd found couldn't have been used for anything in the past few years. With all the holes in its floor, nobody would have been able to transport the number of cattle stolen anywhere.

Amelia Klondike, soon to marry Finn Brannigan, appeared in the entrance with a bright smile on her face. "Good. No one else is here. We have time to talk." Her good friend for years sat down next to Lucy. "What's this I'm hearing about you and Ben being an item, seen together a number of times since he left the hospital?"

Lucy lifted one shoulder in a shrug. "I don't listen to the gossip, so I can't answer that question."

"Don't play innocent with me. Your cheeks are getting red, a sure sign something is going on between you two."

"We are friends." But even as she said that, Lucy knew it was more than that. When he'd kissed her on Sunday at the stream, she felt connected to Ben beyond friendship. He spoke to a need she thought she'd buried after Jesse. "How are the wedding plans coming along?"

Amelia shook her head and sank against the back of the cushioned chair. "I'm not going to tell you a thing if you don't share with me."

Lucy heard the outside door open and bent toward the curly-haired blonde beauty. "Ben and I are friends. Like you and I are."

Amelia burst out laughing as Pastor Mathers came into the room with Ben. He grinned at Lucy and winked, then took a seat at the other end of the table, so every time she glanced up, she saw his face first.

Not half a minute later Ruby entered, slightly out of breath. "Oh, good, I'm not late. Carson's nephew fell off a horse. I wanted to make sure Brandon would be okay before I came."

"Great, everyone is here. Amelia, would you take notes on the meeting?" Lucy asked while Ruby took a chair between the pastor and Ben. "We have a lot to finalize tonight. We'll have one more meeting before the Easter-egg hunt this time next week. Will that be all right with everyone?"

Each member of the committee nodded.

"As y'all know, the Stillwater Ranch will be the location this year for the event. Lucy has filled me in on what has been planned so far, but I'd like to add some things to the festivities." Ben looked right at Lucy. "Instead of the children coming for an hour or so, why don't we make this several hours with more than just hunting for Easter eggs and a few age-appropriate games?"

Lucy groaned inwardly. "At this late date?"

"I thought we could add a couple of things like various races with eggs, an art tent and a reading circle. I saw on the internet the different activities they have at the White House at this time. The Easter Egg Roll is an annual event for kids from all over the United States." Ben looked at each member of the committee. "We have a large tent at the ranch. We have the art teacher from the elementary school in our congregation."

"Maybe next year—"

"Why wait?" Ben interrupted Lucy. "If I learned one thing, it's to seize the moment. One moment I was going to see Carson, the next I was lying on the ground unconscious. I didn't wake up for weeks. We don't know what's going to happen in the future, so why not make each day count? I'll do the extra work."

Stunned, Lucy searched for words to say. Too much was going on.

"I like it, Ben," Amelia said. "We already have the egg hunt, refreshments and a couple of games. The kids are already coming, and it would be fun to add a few more activities. If it's successful, we can think about doing even more next year."

"I'll set up the tent and recruit some teenagers to help with the arts and crafts. I suggested it today to the three girls that work after school at my ranch. They loved the idea. They thought they could get some of the teenage boys in the intern program to help with the races. We could have an egg roll like at the White House, racing with an egg in a spoon and an egg toss, especially for the older children." Ben scanned everyone's faces but Lucy's, as though he wasn't sure of her reaction.

Lucy was warming to the idea. She watched the excitement in Ben's expression, and it was contagious. He'd always played as hard as he worked, but this was different. This was about others. He wasn't thinking of fun for himself but for the children at the egg hunt. Had Ben really changed since the accident? Would it last? Or with all this extra work, would he burn himself out before summer? She didn't want to see that, either.

Pastor Mathers cleared his throat. "I don't see why we don't try Ben's idea, but we'll need to look at the funding."

"No problem. I'll give the money necessary for the supplies," Amelia said with a smile. "We've had so much tension in town the past six months that it would be nice to have a celebration like this for the children."

Lucy took in the faces of each member; the more she looked at Ben the more excited she became. His smile filled the whole conference room. In the past she'd seen glimpses of this new Ben, but he was shining bright right now. "Okay, we have a suggestion for expanding the Easter-egg hunt with three new activities— arts-and-crafts tent, storytelling area and egg races. Is anyone opposed to trying it this year?"

No one said a word.

"Then, it is decided. Ruby, you'll still be in charge of the refreshments, Amelia the egg hunt and now Ben the extra activities. We'll combine the games and races. I can help you since we only have ten days to get it in place." Even Ben had pulled her into the expanded egg hunt. "I can plan the arts-and-crafts activities and the races. Pastor Mathers, will you recruit readers for the storytelling part?"

"I'll volunteer to be one, and I have several others in mind, too."

"Good. Let's finish the rest of the business. I know we're all probably ready to have dinner." Lucy took the next twenty minutes going over the church's youth group running the different age egg hunts and manning the refreshment table, as well as where they could fit in with the expanded plan.

At the end the pastor rose first and skimmed the faces of the committee members. "I have to say I'm excited about the direction this is going. Our advertising is garnering a lot of interest even from the surrounding towns. I'm so glad we've opened it up this year to all children. Our community needs to remember how important love is in the midst of the tempers and accusations flying around. God is love, and I want to spread that word. Thank you for your help."

Amelia angled toward Lucy. "I'll send the notes to your email tomorrow. We need to get together soon. I'm going to catch Pastor Mathers about having Finn read to the children. They always love to see a Texas Ranger. See you."

As Lucy rose, Ben made his way to her. "How about grabbing dinner at Maggie's? We can discuss what we want to do in the art-and-crafts tent. I think I'll turn the races over to Maddy, Lynne and Christie to recruit some of their friends to help. I'm glad you're going to be there, too."

"Everyone will have to chip in to get it done. Why didn't you say something to me about your idea before you announced it?"

"Because you would look at the problems, not the possibilities. You're overworked and the uproar in the community has been stressful for you. I was in a coma a good part of it. So it's not the same for me."

As the rest of the committee filed out of the conference room, Lucy leaned back against the conference table, grasping its edge. "Where are all these ideas coming from? First the camp and now this."

"They've always been in the back of my mind, but I realized when I almost died that I couldn't wait until later to implement them. Later may never come. I talked with Pastor Mathers before the meeting. He likes the idea about having the Vacation Bible School at the Stillwater Ranch, so I'm going forward with it this summer."

"So your new motto is seize the moment?"

"Exactly," he said with a chuckle. "So how about dinner?"

Exhaustion still clung to her, but she couldn't say no to Ben. That adorable grin and twinkle in his eyes told her to seize the moment. "Yes. I'm hungry, and it beats my cooking for once."

"Good, because I don't have one artistic bone in this body. I'm gonna need your help. Maybe the girls should do the arts-and-crafts tent."

"Let's see who they recruit to help, then make the decision who will do what."

"See, you're perfect to run this committee. You know how to delegate."

Warmed by his compliment, Lucy left the church with Ben strolling next to her. The sunlight splashed in brilliant colors of red, orange and yellow across the sky. The air held a crispness as the end of the day neared while a bird chirped in a budding tree nearby. For this moment tranquillity ruled, and she relished it because she knew it wouldn't last.

Ben pulled out the chair at Maggie's Coffee Shop for Lucy, and instead of sitting across from her, he took the one kitty-corner from her.

Abigail handed them the menu and filled their water glasses. "It's nice to see you up and around so much, Ben. There were a lot of people praying you recovered."

He gave her a grin. "Thanks, Abigail. That's what I love about Little Horn. People care about their neighbors."

"Let me know when you're ready to order. Sheriff, I know you like chicken potpie, and that's our specialty tonight." Abigail turned and headed for the kitchen, her black ponytail swishing as she walked.

"Were you including Byron in that statement of neighbors caring?" Lucy closed her menu and set it to the side.

"He blusters a lot, but I do think he cares about the town, just not necessarily his relations."

"You're thinking about his cousin Mac. He was a proud man, and when Byron wouldn't help him, he fell apart one drink at a time and refused some people's attempt to help."

"Pride goeth before destruction. Proverbs has it right. As my relationship deteriorated with my father, I refused to make amends. I knew he was in pain from his back injury. When I was thrown from a bronco my last season on the rodeo circuit, I began to understand what he'd gone through. It took months for my back to heal. By the time I figured out how pain can change a person, my father had been dead a year."

"Personally I don't know why you would want to sit on a bronco just to be thrown off seconds later."

He chuckled. "It's the challenge. I could say personally I don't know why you would strap a gun to your waist and face down criminals."

"Someone has to keep the order."

Ben closed his menu and signaled for Abigail to take their order. "I'm just glad you're back in Little Horn. A city is much more dangerous than here."

"You sound like my father, but I needed to do that. I'm a better law-enforcement officer because of my years on the San Antonio police force. I told my father what was good for him should be good for me."

Abigail paused next to Ben with her pad and pen. "Ready?"

"Yes, I want the chicken potpie and a cup of decaf." Ben looked at Lucy.

"The same."

Abigail wrote down their orders. "Any dessert?"

"Pecan pie with a scoop of vanilla ice cream. How about you, Lucy?"

She shook her head. "A refill of decaf coffee will have to do."

"I'm with you on that, Sheriff. But if I'd lost a lot of weight while sleeping, I'd be ordering what Ben did and enjoy every second of eating the treats." Abigail smiled at him, took the menus and left.

This was the perfect chance for her to champion Abigail as a nanny or… She couldn't quite bring herself to think about Abigail as wife material, but that was what she'd thought last week. "She has a pretty smile. I'm surprised she's still single." Lucy drank her water, watching Ben over the rim of the glass.

"I imagine she hasn't found the right person. For the longest time she was the primary caretaker for her mother."

"But she died last summer. She's a hard worker, kind and loves children. She works in the nursery at church."

"That's right. She was playing with Cody when I picked him up last Sunday from the nursery." Ben took a big sip of his drink.

"You should ask her out. She'll make a man a good wife and—"

He nearly spewed his water, but instead ended up choking on it when it went down the wrong way.

Lucy pounded on his back. "Okay?"

He nodded while his eyes glistened with tears. Slowly he began drawing in deeper breaths. "What are you doing? This is the second person you've talked to me about going on a date with."

"I thought I would help as a friend. You said you needed a nanny or a wife. I was thinking of Abigail at least as a nanny. I can't answer for the other option. Only you."

"I can take care of that myself. If I were interested in her, it would be as a nanny. In fact, thanks for pointing out her work in the nursery. I think I'll talk to her. She would be perfect for that job. It certainly would take care of my immediate problem." Ben realized he'd toyed with trying to find a mother for Cody, but that couldn't be hurried. Lucy was right. Only he could make that decision, and for the first time in his life, he was thinking of it as an option for him. "Enough about me. Let's talk about the arts and crafts."

"I've got just the person to supervise the activities. Candace Quinn. She's a first-grade teacher, and the kids love her. I remember she is very talented with stuff like arts and crafts. You should ask her."

Ben eyed Lucy. What was she up to now? Although Candace might actually be the perfect person for the job. "I'm sure you know her better than I do."

"But this is your project. I'm only helping you, and I've been busy running down the leads. Remember the Robin Hoods, not to mention all the other things that happen in our county."

"Fine. I'll stop by the school tomorrow and see if she can. But just so you know it, I'm busy, too."

After Abigail set their chicken potpies in front of them, Lucy bowed her head and blessed the meal, then lifted her fork. "So Maddy, Christie and Lynne are going to help us in the tent?"

"That's what they said, while a few of their male friends in the intern program will probably do the races. That way it'll give you another opportunity to be around Maddy."

"I appreciate that, but I'm hoping the case will be closed by then."

"That would be nice. Life back to normal in Little Horn rather than neighbors eyeing neighbors with suspicion. It's clear the person has inside information. I've contacted a friend in Dallas, a private investigator. He'll start searching for Betsy in Texas, then move to the surrounding states. Maddy helped me with what Betsy likes and possible jobs she might apply for."

"If I can get enough on the McKay twins and they are the Robin Hoods, will you continue to look for Betsy?"

Ben hadn't thought that far ahead. Maddy had been excited when he'd asked for her help concerning Betsy. But would it be the best for Betsy? "I don't know. Maybe.

She fell through the cracks. We should have done more to help her, especially after her father died."

"But I can see why she left. A fresh start with no one judging who you are by your past and your family is appealing."

"And dealing with her cousins, especially Byron. I have a hard time doing that. I'm beginning to think I wasn't so bad off being in a coma. At least I didn't have to hear Byron's rants and raves like the rest of you."

"With money and power comes responsibility. Byron hasn't figured that out."

After a few bites of his chicken potpie, Ben washed it down with coffee, then said, "Maddy did tell me today she thought Gareth and Winston were upset about Betsy leaving town suddenly last year. Gareth told her he and his brother had been looking for their cousin. They wanted to help her even if their father didn't."

"A good motive for them to steal from Byron, but the other ranchers?"

"All part of the Lone Star Cowboy League, which wouldn't help Mac because he wasn't a member. Byron pushed that through. Technically he was right, but Carson is trying to change that rule. Not easy when Byron and his cronies are balking at it."

"Byron stands behind rules when it's convenient for him."

Hunger satisfied, Ben lounged back in his chair and sipped his coffee. It was nice discussing what was happening in Little Horn with Lucy. He cared about the town, and she did, too. Because he'd been in a coma, he could look at the situation from a more objective mind than the others.

Ben remembered what she said earlier. "So what leads are you running down tomorrow?"

"I'm driving to Austin. There's a jewelry store that sold the music box. Thankfully it's on this side of Austin on the outskirts."

"Why not send a deputy to see if Gareth purchased the music box?"

"I need a break. I'm leaving early, so I should be back early afternoon."

"I hope you'll let me know."

"I'll call you, and you can let me know if Candace will do the arts and crafts for the Easter-egg hunt." Lucy tilted her head to the left and looked toward the right, something Ben had figured out she did when she was thinking about what to do or say. "If she agrees, I think we should meet for dinner with her tomorrow, if she can, and then have a meeting with the teens on Saturday at your ranch."

"Where do you want to have dinner?" He loved seeing her work through a problem and come up with what to do.

"My house. Nothing fancy. Steaks, baked potatoes and salad."

"Are you going to have time for that with going to Austin? Why not come to my ranch for dinner tomorrow night?"

She fixed her gaze on him. "Because I don't want you to accuse me of trying to fix you two up."

"Is that what you're trying to do?"

She slid the last piece of her food into her mouth; again her head tilted to the left. "Okay, Candace would be a great wife and mother for some man. She's been here a few years and fits right in. Kids love her. But I suggested her because she's really good artistically. I did a presentation to her first-grade class about safety, and I saw firsthand all the creative projects her students have done."

"You don't need to do anything. I'm going to approach Abigail tomorrow about being Cody's nanny. If she accepts the job, then there isn't a problem." Even as he said those words, he couldn't dismiss the emptiness he felt, especially when he saw Grady and Chloe together. He wanted the best for his son, and he knew a loving mother could make a difference. But the only one he was even vaguely interested in was Lucy. There was something between them he couldn't describe, nor had he experienced it before. And she'd made it clear she wasn't a contender.

Smiling, Lucy relaxed back. "Well, then, I'm glad I pointed her out to you, and you can have the dinner with Candace and me at your house tomorrow."

Yep, he was definitely attracted to Lucy. She could hold her own with anyone—even Byron. She had dated before she left for San Antonio. Why didn't she go out now? Why didn't she want more in life than being the sheriff? What had happened in San Antonio?

The school secretary told Ben that Candace was in her classroom, eating lunch before her students returned. He paused in the doorway to room number twelve and peered inside. Candace had a sandwich in one hand while staring down at a paper on her desk. She was an attractive woman with short brown hair, a petite frame and large blue eyes.

He took a deep breath and knocked on the doorjamb. Candace glanced up and grinned. "What are you doing here, Ben? I don't think you need to worry just yet about your son and school."

Some of the tension siphoned from him as he headed toward the teacher at her desk. "From what I've heard, when he is ready, I hope he gets you as a first-grade teacher."

"He has a fifty-fifty chance, since there are only two of us. What can I do for you?" She put her sandwich down on a paper napkin.

"I know you don't have much time so I'll make this quick. As you probably know, our church is having the Easter-egg hunt next Saturday at my ranch. I wanted to do a little more for the kids and have suggested an arts-and-crafts tent."

"My class is excited about the event and would love doing something like that."

"Good. Would you be willing to come up with some projects they could do in a short time and be in charge of the tent? I already have some teenagers who want to help."

"I'd told my students I would be there, so why not? Sure, I can do it."

"Great. Lucy and I thought we could meet tonight at the ranch to discuss the event and make sure we have the right supplies. If tonight doesn't work, we can come up with another time."

"Tonight's fine. What time?"

"Six. We'll eat, then talk."

Candace stood and extended her hand, which he shook. "See you then. It'll be a good time to give Chloe and Grady their wedding gift."

"They should be there for dinner." As he left, he remembered their handshake. No sparks had flown when he'd touched her. Nothing. She was a nice lady—but she wasn't Lucy. That crept into his thoughts unexpectedly. His gait faltered momentarily.

Twenty minutes later he arrived at the ranch, checked in to make sure Cody was all right, then walked to the barn. His cell phone rang as he entered. Noting it was Lucy calling, he hurriedly answered it. "Tell me it's good news."

"It is. The staff identified Gareth as the teenager who bought the music box. Get this—for three hundred and fifty dollars, and the necklace was another one hundred and fifty. That's a lot of money for a sixteen-year-old who doesn't work. Byron is rich, but I checked with a source and discovered the boys only get an allowance. It would have taken Gareth months to save the money, not to mention the gifts Maddy received at Christmas from her secret admirer."

"I'm not surprised. Byron is stingy with his money."

"So where did the cash for the gifts come from?"

"Are you going to talk with the twins or Byron?"

"Not yet. I'd like another piece of evidence. What I have is circumstantial. The cattle thief the New Mexico State Police caught isn't involved in our case."

Ben slipped his cell phone into his pocket and went in search of Zed. He remembered being angry with his father, but he'd never considered stealing from the ranch, and certainly not from his neighbors.

Chapter Eight

"You may kiss the bride," Pastor Mathers announced to the small gathering Friday, not long after six.

Ben stood next to his brother, who wrapped his arms around Chloe and kissed his new wife. The whole time through the short ceremony, Ben had been happy for Grady. The smiles on the bride's and groom's faces touched a lonely place in Ben. He wanted that, but no one he'd dated all these years had come close to capturing his love. He wanted someone who would stick by him even through the bad times. He loved his mother, but she'd abandoned his dad when he was dealing with pain. There were always two sides of an issue, and until his coma, he hadn't seen his father's. Pain didn't make it okay to be grumpy and mean most of the time, but it did explain what had happened in their marriage.

When Grady and Chloe parted, their grins encompassed their whole faces. Ben couldn't help but do the same. His gaze latched on to Lucy's. In his eyes her beauty surpassed Chloe's. He didn't get that many chances to see her in a dress, but the pale green of her outfit made her eyes stand out.

She broke eye contact and hugged Chloe. "I'm so excited for you."

"Thanks." Chloe turned to Grandma Mamie and enveloped her in her embrace. "I appreciate all you've done to make me feel a part of the Stillwater family." Then she swept around and looked right at him. "I'm glad you have recovered. We didn't want to get married without you here."

Ben nodded. "I aim to please."

"So when are you going to get hitched?" Grady asked in the sanctuary.

"I was just waiting. You know how you like to be first, big brother." Ben clapped Grady on his back. "Enough of this. Let's go celebrate. Martha Rose, Eva and Grandma have been working for the past few days on this shindig."

Grady and Chloe led the wedding party out of the church. At Grady's car, he opened the door for Chloe. "We may just take the long way home."

Mamie stopped next to Ben. "No, you aren't. You have a lifetime with Chloe. You have guests waiting at the ranch to congratulate y'all."

Ben could tell by the barely contained grin that Grady had said that just to tease their grandmother. "If you don't show up, I'll eat your share, so don't worry, none of the food will go to waste. Grandma, you can ride with Lucy and me." He'd picked Lucy up earlier, insisting it was his duty to make sure the maid of honor got to the church on time.

"I'm going with Pastor Mathers. Someone has to keep him company on the drive."

As Grady and Chloe drove out of the parking lot, Ben turned to Lucy. "My chariot awaits." He swept his arm toward his truck, at least cleaned with no signs of the dust and dirt from the day before.

"I could have driven myself." Lucy strolled toward his vehicle.

"The least I could do for the wedding party is pick you up and take you home. Don't worry. This is not a date."

She looked at him over the hood of his truck. "I know, and I wasn't worried. More like preoccupied."

"Why?"

"Yesterday the Oklahoma State Police informed me they brought in an illegal cattle broker with ties to Texas. They're offering him a deal today to talk. I'm hoping he takes it and puts an end to the Robin Hoods."

"When will you know?"

"Sometime in the next couple of days."

"Then, we'll have to really celebrate. Of course, if it's Byron's twins, we all may be in for a long spring. It makes me feel sorry for those boys. Now that I'm a father, I'm aware of how important it is for me to set a good example for my son."

"We can both agree that Byron hasn't." Lucy climbed into the front passenger seat.

"For tonight, no thoughts of work. Chloe is so good for Grady. I'm getting used to him being around. I'm hoping they'll stay, and we can work together. There's so much I'd like to do."

"Are you sure you weren't plotting all these projects while in a coma?"

While he left Little Horn and drove in the direction of the ranch, he slid a glance to her. "I have a lot of time to make up for." Ben looked out the rearview mirror at

Pastor Mathers following in his car. "You do know what Grandma is doing, right?"

Lucy peered over her shoulder. "Playing matchmaker."

"Yep."

"I'll just have to let her know we're only friends."

"Are we?"

He felt her eyes drilling into him but kept his attention on the highway before him.

"I thought we were friends. Has something happened?"

He pulled off the road onto the shoulder, switched off the engine, then angled toward her. "I think there is more, not less. What's between us feels nothing like it did in high school."

Lucy's eyes grew round.

Pastor Mathers slowed his car, and Ben rolled down his window at the same time Grandma did hers.

"Do you need help?" Mamie asked, a gleam of mischief barely contained by a straight face.

"We're fine. We'll be along in a minute."

"That's okay. I can take care of the guests at the ranch." She winked at him.

Ben barely contained his laughter at his grandmother's tactics. "We'll be there soon." When the pastor pulled away, Ben turned back to Lucy. "Can you deny something is different between us?"

"I think our friendship has grown recently, but I'm not interested in anything else."

"I'm not the same person."

She snapped her fingers as she said, "Just like that, you've changed."

"It happens. Look at the story of Paul."

"I can see you love Cody, but is he your new pet project? Will it last? For years you resisted putting down any roots, but now you want to?"

"My roots have always been here. Stillwater Ranch has expanded since I took over managing it. That wouldn't have happened without my being serious about my work."

"I know how you feel about your family ranch, but relationships with people are different. If you want one, you have to be willing to commit to it as much as you do to the ranch."

Again Ben wondered what had happened in San Antonio to make Lucy so wary and cynical. He wanted to ask but wasn't sure how. "I've committed to my son. I want to be the best dad I can be, and I know that won't always be easy to do. I've seen too many father/son relationships that fell apart. At least now I know it wasn't all my dad's fault. We both worked at tearing down the bond we once had."

She shifted around, so they faced each other. "That's it. Relationships take a lot of hard work. A person has to be willing to put the time and energy into it and not hightail it the first sign of trouble."

Like he usually had done in the past. "Did that happen to you?"

Half a minute passed, and Ben forgot to breathe as he waited for her to answer.

"Yes. I fell in love with an FBI agent I'd met while working. We dated for a year—the last six months exclusively—and had even been talking about getting married. But I discovered I wasn't the only woman he was seeing and spinning that story to. Jesse wasn't satisfied with one. He needed three in his life. He shuffled his time between us, but all that juggling caught up with him. When I discovered his other two, we met and learned he had spun the same tale for each of us. We confronted him, and I decided to leave San Antonio. After six years, I came back to Little Horn. I'm not a big-city gal."

"See, we have that in common. I can't imagine living in a big city. I don't even need to leave to know that." He reached and grasped her hands. "I'm sorry for what that guy did three years ago. I've always been up front with my intentions. The women I dated knew I wasn't looking for a serious relationship. The truth will always find a way to come out."

She leaned toward him and kissed his cheek. "We'd better get to the celebration before your grandmother comes back for us."

"Hardly. She's hoping we'll stay here," he said with a chuckle.

Ben started the truck and pulled out onto the highway. At least now he knew why she was leery of any relationship. If he was honest with himself, he couldn't blame her for feeling that way about him. For years, he'd tried his best to stay single with no obligations except to the ranch. Now he had to face the consequences of that behavior.

As the hour grew late, Lucy stood back from the crowd at Stillwater Ranch and sipped her punch while she watched the expressions on the guests' faces. Ben's house was big enough that it could accommodate more than fifty people at the wedding celebration. Chloe looked beautiful in her ivory-colored silk dress, and her face glowed, especially when she was with Grady.

I want that. I want to look at someone with love and have it returned. I want a family. Those thoughts flitted through Lucy's mind as she took in the joy. How had Chloe let go of the fear Grady would end up like her first husband? Chloe had known Grady most of her life, but Lucy had first worked with Jesse, then dated him for months before she'd fallen in love with him. She'd thought she knew him well and that he would never cheat on her, like some of the people she'd worked with. Sure, Chloe had an unborn baby to think about, but still... *How do you know if it's forever?*

Amelia planted herself next to Lucy. "I'm so glad to see Chloe happily married. Grady will be a great dad for her baby. Remember when we used to talk about who was going to get married first? You were to supposed to marry before me, not be the last holdout."

"I've got three weeks before you walk down the aisle."

"And who are you pursuing?" Amelia asked with a chuckle.

"That is a problem. Just dodging Byron has taken all my extra time."

"Are you close to apprehending someone?"

Lucy turned toward her friend. "Yes, but until I have the evidence, I'm not accusing anyone. We've had enough people being accused without good evidence."

"I agree. Ruby's brother, Derek, was a good example of some people pushing for a solution without any proof. Speaking of that, where is Byron?"

"I don't think he was invited. Chloe told me she didn't want anything to spoil her day."

"Good for her, but that may make things dicey for Grady and Ben."

"What will be dicey?" Ben asked as he joined them.

"Not inviting Byron." Amelia waved to her fiancé, Finn, who wove his way through the crush of people toward them.

"He'll have two Stillwaters to go through if he makes a ruckus about it. It's time we stand up to him. He's a bully. No wonder his sons have that reputation, too. He may have the largest ranch in this part of Texas, but he can't plow through everyone in his way."

Finn put his arm around Amelia's waist. "If you need help, I'm with you."

"I imagine the next Lone Star Cowboy League meeting will be interesting. I hope by then I'll know where Betsy is. I want to persuade her to return to Little Horn." Ben moved close to Lucy, goose bumps appearing on her arms.

"That won't set well with Byron." Amelia glanced at Finn. "We had a great time tonight. Thanks, Ben, for opening your home to us. I'm looking forward to next Saturday with the Easter-egg hunt and festivities."

"We're meeting with the teens tomorrow to work out the setup in the tent and the races. I have to say I'm getting excited." Ben shook Finn's hand and then he and Amelia walked off together.

"I'm glad Amelia found Finn. She's always giving to others. It's nice to see her happy. She deserves it." Lucy couldn't keep the wistful tone from her voice.

"And so do you." He clasped her hand and drew her away from the crowd. "Lately I've seen how hard you work, putting in long hours, and the thanks you get is Byron accusing you of not doing your job. Have you heard anything from the Oklahoma State Police yet?" Ben stepped in front of her, blocking her from the guests around them.

"No, but I'll let you know when I do. I want this settled, but if it's the McKay twins, I don't look forward to telling Byron."

"That's why I think you're right about getting the evidence first. Byron won't make it easy for you or anyone."

She needed to change the subject. She was so tired of thinking about the Robin Hoods case. It affected so many people in the county, especially around here. "I can't believe how Maddy managed to get Cody to go to bed. He was loving all the attention. I have a feeling you're gonna have your hands full with him."

Ben's expression brightened, his eyes twinkling. "Takes after his dad. A real charmer."

Laughing, she shook her head. "Incorrigible is more like it."

"Who me? Never. I'm a guy who goes with the flow."

Lucy cocked her head to the side and thought about how he'd been through the years. "Yeah, you're right. I have to admit it has been easy working with you the past few weeks, and the plans for the Easter-egg hunt are turning out to be much better. The kids have always enjoyed it every year, but this one will be special. I'm glad you woke up."

He placed his hand flat on the wall behind her and leaned close. "So am I. I feel as if I've been given a new life."

"When I returned to Little Horn three years ago, I felt like that." Normally when someone stepped into her personal space, she got defensive. So many suspects had over the course of her career, she'd become protective of that space. But Ben didn't make her feel like that. Maybe because she had known him for years and knew where he stood—or did she?

Carson approached and slapped Ben on the back. "I've already told Grady good-night, but I wanted to tell you if you need help with the Easter-egg hunt, I'll pitch in. Ruby will be coming early, so I might as well."

"Sounds good," Ben said, moving next to Lucy, "but work on your timing next time."

Carson shifted his gaze to Lucy, then back to Ben. "Ah, so all the rumors are correct. Want to tell me anything?"

What rumors?

"Yeah, get lost." Ben chuckled.

Heat scored her face as though the sun had burned her skin. "I'll leave you two to work it out." She slipped between the two men and made her way toward Chloe who was talking to Amelia.

Lucy pulled the two women off to the side. "Do either of you know about the rumors going around town about Ben and me? And if so, why didn't you tell me?"

Chloe exchanged a look with Amelia, then said, "Do you mean the one about y'all dating?"

"But we're not."

"He brought you here tonight." Amelia pressed her lips together as if she was trying not to smile.

"I was Chloe's maid of honor. He was the best man. It seemed logical…" She'd let Ben steamroller her into coming with him, just like dinner the other night at Maggie's Coffee Shop. "Okay, I can see how some busybodies might get the idea we're dating, but I need you to set them straight. We're on a couple of committees together. That's all."

"Why should you care?" Amelia asked. "You and Ben have always been part of the rumor mill. When you two are together, sparks fly."

"They do not! Okay, maybe because he makes me exasperated at times."

"Yeah, sure." Chloe grinned.

Grady joined them, placing his arm around Chloe and bringing her close to his side. "I'm stealing my wife. We need to leave. We still have to drive to Austin."

"When will you be back from your honeymoon?" As Lucy stared at Grady, she saw Ben for a few seconds. It was disconcerting, especially in light of what people were saying about her and Ben.

"Tuesday. We're spending a few days away from Little Horn, but it isn't our official honeymoon. That'll come later when things settle down." Grady looked lovingly at Chloe.

"Let me know when that'll be." As if staking a claim to Lucy, Ben stopped beside her, so close their arms grazed each other.

"Do you have your bag packed?" Grady asked Chloe.

She nodded. "Already in the car."

"Then, let's go."

Ben whistled and raised his arms. "Everyone, the bride and groom are leaving."

Cheers and clapping thundered through the room.

Grady took Chloe's hand and headed for the front door with everyone congratulating them again.

Ben took Lucy's hand. "Don't let the gossipmongers get to you. Half the stuff they spread around is wrong."

"Half? That doesn't change the fact we are the topic of conversations. Byron will find a way to use that against me. To him a sheriff is not allowed to have a life outside the job."

Ben glanced down at Lucy. "Is that why you work so hard?"

"Why do *you* work so hard?"

"Because I like to."

"That's my answer, too. I grew up knowing I would be a police officer. I don't just arrest people. I help them, too. That's fulfilling."

"C'mon. Wait till you see what Zed and the other ranch hands did to Grady's car." He tugged her toward the crowd walking outside to watch the couple leave.

Lucy broke out laughing when she saw the car in the glow of the porch lights. "It looks like a float in a parade." She took in all the streamers tied onto everything possible.

Grady spun about, his gaze zeroing in on Ben. "Just you wait."

Then Ben's brother helped Chloe into the front seat, rounded the hood and climbed in behind the steering wheel. Half a minute later, the multicolored car was heading for the highway, with two yards of empty cans bouncing around behind them, clanging together.

"I have a feeling he'll pull over soon and cut that rope with the cans," Ben murmured in her ear.

Chills zipped down her body. Tonight would fuel the gossipmongers, and there wasn't much she could do about it.

Shortly after Grady and Chloe left, the other guests began departing. Mamie stood at the door with Ben, saying goodbye to each one.

When the house was empty of guests, Lucy asked Ben's grandmother, "Can I help you clean up?"

"Don't worry about it. Maddy stayed after putting Cody to bed to help Martha Rose in the kitchen." Mamie swept her arm to indicate the living room. "This can wait until tomorrow. Go home. I don't know about you, but this has been a long day."

Lucy started to insist she could help when Ben placed his hand at the small of her back, nudging her toward him.

Outside as he walked toward his truck, he said, "I've learned not to argue with Grandma. If you stayed to clean, she would, too."

"I can come earlier tomorrow to help before we meet with the girls."

"No, I'll do a lot of it after she goes to bed."

"You do housework?"

When Ben sat behind the steering wheel, he finally answered, "I pitch in where needed, but I draw the line at cleaning windows."

Her laughter died when Lucy remembered Jesse not even taking his dishes to the sink after they ate, let alone helping to clean up after she fixed him dinner. "I'm impressed."

He threw her a glance as he pulled away from the house. "As I've said before, I aim to please."

"I'm not sure I can think of you as a peacemaker, but definitely a mischief maker."

"Who, me? No way."

"How about those times you teased me or tried to rile me in some way?"

"Okay, maybe a little, and I don't do my share of the chores around the house to make peace but to help. My grandmother and Martha Rose work hard to keep the house going. It's a big place. But I won't complain if someone takes over for me in that department."

"Are you hinting at turning around and going back so I can?"

With his eyebrows raised, he said, "Who, me?" then chuckled.

She playfully punched his upper arm. "It was a nice wedding. Small is good."

"Is that what you want?"

"I haven't really thought about it. I'm not serious about anyone. That probably needs to come first." And yet as she said that, she began to doubt the truth to those words. Ben was charming and attractive, but he also was a rogue. She didn't need that in her life. That was what had drawn her to Jesse and look where it got her.

"I thought all girls had their wedding planned by sixteen."

"Where did you get that idea?"

"Oh," he shrugged. "I don't know. Eva?"

Fifteen minutes later, he pulled into Lucy's driveway and started to get out of the truck.

"You don't have to walk me to the door. I've got my gun in my purse."

"You're kidding! At a wedding and dinner party!"

"I got in the habit of taking my weapon everywhere in San Antonio, and there were a couple of times I was glad I did."

"Any time while in Little Horn?" Ben exited the truck.

"Not yet, but it would be too late when the time came and I wasn't prepared."

He strolled beside her to the porch, but when she reached for her key, he clasped her arm and stopped her. Taking a few feet toward her, he stepped into her personal space. She remained where she was, her heartbeat accelerating, her throat going dry. With one of his large hands cupping the side of her face, he tilted it up. His lips hovered an inch from hers. Her breathing ceased—one, two, three seconds before he lay claim to her mouth, covering it with his.

Her knees went weak, and she grasped his shoulders as his hand slid through her hair. She'd been kissed before, but nothing like this.

When he pulled away a few inches, he rested his forehead against hers and cradled her face in both hands. "I couldn't resist. You are beautiful, caring. You deserve happiness."

She couldn't think of anything to say. All she could focus on was the movement of his mouth as he talked, the warmth of his hands against her skin, the woodsy-scented aftershave teasing her nose.

"I'd better let you go to sleep. We have a long day of planning tomorrow. See you at ten." Ben backed away. "But I'm not leaving until you're safely inside."

She held up her purse. "Remember the gun."

"Don't care." He pointed to the floor of the porch. "Not moving until you go inside."

She fumbled for her keys in her purse, her fingers brushing against her gun. Hurriedly she let herself into her house, hearing through the wood, "Good night, Lucy." The words penetrated her defensive wall around her heart, but more than that, his kiss had left her changed—uncertain.

Ben stood out on his front porch, the day promising to be a gorgeous one. In the seventies and not a cloud in the sky. But what really brightened his day was that Lucy was coming. He glanced at his watch. In the next few minutes.

He should be exhausted. He'd slept very little last

night. There was something about their kiss that had left him different. He'd done it on an impulse, but the sensations it had created in him had taken him by surprise. All he could think about was kissing her again.

Her sheriff's SUV turned into the ranch entrance and headed toward him. As he watched, his pulse sped up, and a smile graced his lips. But even more, he looked forward to seeing her. She wasn't like other women he'd known. She was special.

When she parked in the front, he descended the steps and handed her a fresh cup of coffee he'd brought for her. "Good morning. The girls are cleaning the stalls. They'll come to the house when the guys show up."

"Who?"

"Gareth, Rob and Kent."

"Gareth is part of the intern program?"

"No, but Maddy asked him. I couldn't say no to it." He offered his hand. "C'mon in. Grandma Mamie hoped you would join her in the living room before the teenagers come up to the house to talk about the Easter-egg hunt."

"She did? Why?"

"Beats me. I thought I would go to the barn and hurry them along. But I think she's in a matchmaking mode. Just a warning."

"Benjamin Stillwater, don't you go—" The ring of Lucy's cell phone cut her words off.

She quickly answered it and turned her back to Ben. After listening to the person on the other end, she said, "I'll be there Monday morning. This is great news." When she pivoted toward him, excitement glowed on her face. "That was the Oklahoma State Police. Mark Ballard accepted the deal, and he is willing to talk about who he had as clients. He has ties to this area."

Chapter Nine

A weight seemed to lift from Lucy's shoulders as she faced Ben to tell him about the break in the case. "I'll drive to Lawton, Oklahoma, on Monday to get his statement. This may be what I've been looking for. If Ballard can ID Gareth and Winston, then I can arrest them for stealing cattle at the very least."

"Who is this Mark Ballard?" Ben sipped his coffee and headed for his front porch.

"Apparently a legit cattle broker who does illegal deals on the side. From what the Oklahoma State Police said he has some associates in this part of Texas. They had been keeping an eye on him until they had enough evidence to arrest him. They want to shut him down, but they also want the cattle rustlers selling to him, so that's why the authorities are offering him a deal. While I'm there, I'll see if he has bought any cattle from others in the county, although I think the most recent rustling has been by the Robin Hoods."

"Interesting. I wonder how the Robin Hoods knew about him."

"That will be a question I'll ask them when I finally

get to interview them. I remember this time last year one of Byron's ranch hands stole five cattle from him. Maybe the twins overheard something. Thankfully we caught the guy before he could sell them. I have a feeling both Gareth and Winston know a lot of what goes on around here, especially at their father's ranch."

"Having lived under a heavy-handed tyrant, I feel sorry for the boys."

Lucy mounted the steps to the porch. "But you didn't steal from others."

"I had Grandma Mamie to rein me in. I often wonder what I would have done without her. She has kept this family together and been a great example of how you should live. I don't think Byron's wife would stand up to him. My grandmother did with Dad when she thought she should."

Lucy's heart broke as she listened to Ben talk about his relationship with his father. She cherished hers with her dad. "So you think we should give the boys a break?"

"I didn't say that. Grandma never intervened when I deserved a consequence from my actions. If Gareth and Winston did it, they should pay, but as juveniles. I know some will want the book thrown at them because of Byron. He isn't a loved man. But that shouldn't color the decision against Gareth and Winston either way."

"I thought the stealing split the town down the middle, between the ones who benefited from the Robin Hoods and the ones who didn't. This may be worse." The scent of coffee enticed her finally to take a long drink. "This is delicious. Did you make it?"

"Not if I don't have to. My coffee is never like Mamie's."

After another sip, Lucy said, "Ultimately the charges will be up to the DA."

"You can't tell me you don't have input with him."

"Yes. What do you think is fair?"

"Tried in juvenile court. Maybe juvenile detention until eighteen, then some kind of probation at least until they are twenty-one. They need counseling. They need ways to channel their anger, because if they stole from their father, they are two angry teens who need help to see the right path."

The fervent tone of Ben's voice made Lucy wonder if he was partially speaking from experience. Had he turned his anger into playing recklessly and having fun? "You aren't Gareth and Winston" slipped out of her mouth uncensored.

His eyes grew round, his mouth dropped open. "I wasn't talking about me."

"Are you sure you weren't thinking about your teenage years?"

He stared off to the side, his forehead furrowing. When he looked back at her, whatever he'd been wrestling with had been resolved. "Maybe I was. I had some intense feelings concerning my dad. Most of the time I thought he hated me, so I hated him. But now I see I was wrong. It wasn't hate I felt for him but anger. He was hurting physically and emotionally and lashed out at the people closest to him. Grady left. I didn't, so I got the brunt of it."

"Maybe your father needed counseling to deal with the pain."

"Probably. But that is behind me. I'm not letting that influence me now. It did for too many years." He pivoted and opened the front door as though he was signaling the topic of conversation was off-limits. "Cody is walking along the furniture more each day. Wait till you see him."

When Lucy entered the living room, Cody stood at the couch and sidestepped down its length. She went to Mamie and gave her a hug. "Has he exhausted you yet?"

"Give him another hour. I asked Maddy to help me after church tomorrow. Too bad she isn't older. She would be a perfect nanny." Mamie sank against the cushion. "When are the kids going to be here?"

Ben checked his watch before he bent down to pick Cody up. "Fifteen minutes or so. If you have anything to do, Grandma, please do. I'll watch Cody, even during the meeting."

"If you're sure. There's always something to do around here. When will you go to the barn?" Mamie pushed herself to her feet, her movement slower than usual.

No doubt, the wedding preparations on top of an eight-month-old baby in the house were taking its toll on Mamie.

"I have a new horse being delivered today. I want to be there for her arrival. Her foals will bring in some good money for us. I need to make sure she settles in all right. For a mare she is high-strung. It'll be at two."

"Although Cody will be napping most likely at that time, I'm gonna call the ladies at church and tell them I can't make Bible study today."

"No, Mamie. You should go. I can watch Cody while Ben is dealing with his new horse," Lucy offered.

Ben's grandmother shook her head. "I can't ask you to hang around that long."

"I don't mind. It's probably only going to be an hour

or so after the teens leave." Lucy wrapped her arms around the older woman. "You go. Have fun and enjoy yourself. We'll take care of things here."

When Mamie pulled back, a light brightened her eyes, and the tired lines around them didn't seem as deep. "Thank you, child."

As his grandmother left the living room, Ben came to her side, still holding Cody. "I can wake up my son and take him to the barn or have Maddy come up and look after him while I have to be gone. You don't have to do it."

"I know. I want to. Being with Cody reminds me of all the good things in life, and as a police officer, that's a nice feeling to remember." She stroked Cody's back as the baby started to wiggle in his daddy's arms.

Ben's son stopped his restless movements and looked at her. Cody held his arms out and leaned toward her.

Ben passed his baby to Lucy. "He likes you. He doesn't do that to everyone."

"I'm glad. It'll make it easier if he wakes up and sees me this afternoon."

The bell rang and Ben strolled toward the front door to answer it. Lucy cuddled Cody to her because she knew when the teens came into the living room, he'd be curious about them and want to check them out. His scent of baby powder and lotion stirred a dream she'd locked away when Jesse betrayed her. She'd wanted children.

"Look who's here. Cody, my little man, did you sleep well last night?" Maddy took the baby from Lucy and hugged him. "He's wonderful to watch," she continued to say to Lynne and Christie.

Ben came into the living room with Gareth, Kent and Rob right behind him. Gareth's gaze sought Maddy, and as they sat to start the meeting, he rarely took his eyes off her.

After everyone was settled and Cody was showing them how he could walk holding on to a piece of furniture or their hand, Lucy knew she needed to find a way to talk to Gareth without seeming as if it was part of her job.

Ninety minutes later, Ben put his pad down. "I think we've covered everything about next Saturday. If each one of you can recruit another teen to help, we should have enough helpers with the arts-and-crafts tent and the races. Any questions?"

"Are we using hard-boiled eggs in the races?" Gareth sat cross-legged on the floor and tried to persuade Cody to come to him.

"Yes for the younger kids, but for the older ones the eggs will be raw. It makes it more fun." Ben watched as his son, at the end of the couch with one hand on the cushion, assessed Gareth and the distance to him. Cody released his hand, wobbled, then grabbed onto the sofa.

Sitting next to Ben, Lucy nudged his leg and pointed to his son. "It won't be long. He wants to go so badly."

"Yeah, I know." To the group Ben said, "We'll need you here an hour before the Easter-egg hunt starts. I'll have the tent set up, but there will be some last-minute things to do. Okay?"

Everyone responded with a yes or a nod.

Grandma Mamie stepped into the living room. "We have refreshments in the kitchen. I hope y'all stay and enjoy them. Nothing much. Just some pizza, Cokes and chocolate-chip cookies."

His grandmother knew what people enjoyed eating.

As the teenagers followed Grandma to the kitchen, Ben grabbed Cody and trailed after the group. He came up behind Lucy and whispered, "Are you going to talk to Gareth?"

"Only with the group. I'm gonna ask you about Betsy and see where it leads the conversation."

After the teens and Lucy filled their plates with pizza and cookies, they sat in the kitchen at the large table that held eight people and dug in.

Mamie took Cody. "I'll feed him and put him down while you eat."

Ben dished up some food and joined the rest, taking the last place. "I have another project I hope y'all can help me with." When they looked at him, he continued, "The Little Horn sign has been recovered and been returned to where it belongs, but the area around it is weedy and overgrown. I'd like to have the students in the intern program take it on as a project. I thought I would bring it up at the Lone Star Cowboy League meeting, but in the meantime, this afternoon after my mare is delivered, I'm going to the sign with my interns and whoever else wants to. We can at least mow the weeds and grass, then if any of you want, we could finish planting some flowers and shrubs tomorrow."

Maddy grinned. "I love that idea. I'm in for tomorrow, too."

"I can't. We're going to see my grandfather in the nursing home in Austin after church," Lynne said.

"I can." Gareth picked up a slice of pepperoni pizza. "And I'll get Winston to help."

Ben slid a glance toward Lucy. "How about you?"

"Sounds great."

"I'll help today and tomorrow," Rob said, quickly followed by Christie.

Kent frowned. "Sorry, I can't either day, but it's about time we got our sign back. I think our rival school took it. Why would the Robin Hoods do that and then bring it back?"

"We checked into that when it happened during football seasons. If someone at Blue Creek High School did, they have kept it awfully quiet. Same with the other schools we have a big rivalry with." Lucy took a swallow of her drink. "That reminds me, Ben, have you had any success in finding Betsy?"

"You're looking for my cousin?" Gareth asked, his eyebrows raised.

"Yes. I want to make sure she's all right. Do you know where she might be, Gareth? Or any of you?" Ben shifted his gaze from one teen to the next, ending with Gareth. "Maybe we can help her even from afar if she needs it. She left so suddenly."

Sitting next to Gareth, Maddy turned toward him. "Didn't you tell me you and your brother tried to find her?"

His grip on his fork tightened, his knuckles whitening. "We tried. She disappeared," Gareth said, then under his breath muttered, "Thanks to my dad."

Ben wasn't sure exactly what he heard, but Lucy sat across from the teen and might have heard it clearer. "I'm glad my brother has returned to Little Horn. Family is special. It takes them being gone sometimes for us to appreciate them in our lives." As he said that, Ben realized he meant every word. It didn't make any difference what kind of relationship or problems he and Grady had had in the past. It was what they did from here on out.

Maddy stared at her empty plate. "Sometimes it takes you losing them to—" she paused, swiping her hand across her eyes, keeping her head down as she finished "—realize how important they are to you."

Gareth touched her arm, then took her hand, his jaw-line sharp as though he was wrestling with himself about saying something.

Using her napkin, Maddy dabbed her eyes. "Sorry to get all down. This is the month my parents died in a car crash." She raised her head. "But the Derrings are good foster parents."

Uncomfortable with the silence, Ben grabbed the plate of cookies and took one. "Anyone else want dessert? I know our cook makes the best in the county."

Rob took one and passed it to Kent. "I totally agree."

Lynne asked the group about the spring dance coming up. Who was going? The girls began chattering about it while the boys remained quiet, but Gareth didn't let go of Maddy's hand.

Later when Ben walked the teenagers to the door and thanked them, he watched Gareth stroll with Maddy toward the barn, off from the others. The young man slid his arm around her shoulder. If he was one of the Robin Hoods, he hated to think what kind of uproar would occur when the town found out. He felt for the twins. He sensed smoldering anger barely held in check under the surface.

"I'm more convinced than ever he and Winston are the Robin Hoods." Lucy came up behind him and stood in the doorway with Ben.

"I'm afraid you're right."

"You don't sound happy the problem plaguing us for months will finally be over soon."

Ben faced Lucy. "I was much like Gareth when I was his age."

"No, you weren't. He and his brother often bully when they don't get their way. Or so I've heard. No one will come forward against them. You weren't like that."

"I used the rodeo activities I did to get rid of my anger toward my father. That helped me, but I still did things I'm not proud of. I see the potential in Gareth. He really cares for Maddy in spite of what his father would say if he knew. He's here helping with the Easter-egg hunt and the town sign."

"Because Maddy asked him."

"But he got into the planning like everyone else. I could tell he enjoyed himself."

Lucy clasped his arms and gazed at him with a softness in her eyes. "This is why you're good working with kids. I'm glad you're thinking of expanding what you already do."

Her words washed over him and lifted his spirits more than winning the championship at the rodeo. "Thank you. That means a lot to me."

He wanted to kiss her. Awareness he was standing in the doorway with a partial view of the barn didn't deter him. Lifting her chin, he looked into her beautiful eyes that sparkled, then bent his head toward hers. Their lips touched, a gentle kiss that quickly evolved into a deep one that made Ben realize he would never think of Lucy as only a friend. In that moment their relationship changed.

When he drew back to look at her, her face glowed, much like he felt inside. The moment hung between them, neither saying a word.

Until a cry resounded through the house at the same time a truck hauling a horse trailer came toward the barn.

Lucy glanced outside, then said, "I'll get Cody. You go see to your horse."

"They're early."

"That just means we can go take care of the sign early." Lucy hurried toward the back of the house where Grandma Mamie had put Cody down to sleep.

Lucy had been trying to set Ben up with others when she was the one he was interested in. She was caring, someone he could share himself with, and whenever he saw her with children, she was a natural with them. He started for the barn, whistling the song "The Yellow Rose of Texas."

When Lucy arrived at the location of the town sign off the highway, it looked as if she was the last one to come. Gareth, Winston and Rob were unloading the back of Ben's and their trucks while Maddy, Christie and Ben were putting up a border around the sign, leaving an area of six feet square to plant bushes and flowers.

Lucy parked on the shoulder behind the pickup and approached Ben, who was digging a place for the border while the girls set up the interlocking stone pieces. "Sorry, I'm late. I had to go into the station and take care of a problem."

Ben stopped and smiled. "I thought Sunday was your day off."

"In my dreams. Remember, 24/7. A rancher in Blue Creek reported some cattle missing, but as I was driving toward his place, he found them in the field one over. Apparently when he was searching, they were sitting down under a tree and a small raise in the land blocked his view."

Ben's gaze skimmed down her length. "You didn't even get a chance to change."

Lucy still had on the clothes she had worn to church, a blue dress and flats. "Nowadays when I hear cattle are missing, I go right away." Off to her side, she noticed Gareth laying the bag of river rocks by the border near her, his attention drifting to Ben and her when she'd mentioned that cattle were gone. "I thought by the time I went home and changed, you all would be almost finished."

"Tell you what. While we finish the border, why don't you arrange where we should plant the bushes and flowers?"

"I've got some boots in my trunk." Lucy traipsed to her Mustang, retrieved her boots and returned ready to do what she could. "Who donated the plants?"

"Carson and me."

"Our dad took care of the rocks, and Lynne's dad bought the edging for the border," Winston said as he put down the last sack. "So where do you want us to dig a hole for these?" He gestured toward the bushes.

"The ones that grow taller ought to go in first." Gareth grabbed one bucket with a shrub. "I think this Texas purple sage should go near the sign. Its flowers through the summer will add color and allow the sign to stand out."

"Have you done landscaping before?" Lucy asked.

"Yes, at the ranch."

Surprised the boy had, Lucy decided to work with Gareth laying out the plants where they would go. Then they all stepped back to take a look. "I like this. Gareth, you have a good eye."

"I'm glad *you* appreciate it."

The way the teenage boy stressed the word *you* made her wonder who hadn't appreciated his work. "I sure do. A pretty garden makes a drab place look good."

"Tell that to my dad," Gareth mumbled, snatched up a shovel and started digging the first hole.

When the border was completed, the girls planted the flowers. Ben stepped back to watch the five teens work. "We should be through soon."

"I wish I could have done more. In fact, Gareth is the one who really arranged everything." She lowered her voice and asked, "Byron really donated the river rocks?"

"Yeah, surprised me when Gareth told me yesterday. They brought the rocks in their truck and were waiting for me to come. If we need more, Gareth said he would bring more."

Lucy turned her back to the group and whispered, "Do you think they have regretted what they did—that is, if they are the Robin Hoods?"

"Possibly. I hope you'll call me after you meet with Ballard tomorrow. Will you arrest them when you get back or wait?"

"It'll depend on the time. If not, the next day after school. I don't want to make a scene at school."

"I understand. If you poke the grizzly, it gets madder."

"No, that's not it. I don't think anything I do will make Byron happy. You're rubbing off on me. When I look at them from your perspective, I see them differently."

"Nothing is black-and-white." Still holding his shovel, Ben glanced beyond Lucy. "Can I help you, Winston?"

"Yeah, Gareth wanted to make sure if you like the placing of the holly bushes or if they should come out more."

Lucy turned toward the teen and noticed the progress made. "Maybe half a foot at most. We'll probably have to trim the shrubs every spring. It looks really nice. We should have done this a long time ago."

"I guess our break time is over." Ben moved toward the bushes still in buckets off to the side and grabbed one to plant.

Lucy remembered a towel she had in the backseat of her Mustang and retrieved it. Using it to kneel on, she helped Maddy and Christie finish putting the flowers in the ground.

An hour later the garden was finished with the last bag of river rocks dumped and spread out. The group stood back to see how it looked from a distance.

"Beautiful, even without all the flowers blooming yet." Holding his hand, Maddy stood next to Gareth, who smiled from ear to ear.

"Yeah, I agree," Gareth said, looking at Maddy as though the rest of them weren't even there.

Winston poked his brother in the ribs. "That's Dad coming."

Lucy peered at the truck barreling down the highway. She wished she had her radar gun to clock him, especially when Byron came to a screeching halt, slammed out of his vehicle and marched toward them.

Now what? Lucy had had about enough with Byron. She stepped toward him.

He bypassed her and halted in front of his twin sons. "I didn't give you permission to take the river rocks out of the shed."

"I left a note telling you." Winston backed away a few paces while his brother stayed still.

"Yeah, I know. Why do you think I'm here?"

Gareth squared his shoulders and fisted his hands. "You want them back? It's for the town."

Red-faced, Byron looked at the garden and finally realized everyone was staring at him and his sons. "Just because you left a note you were taking them doesn't make it all right."

"We'll pay for them." Winston stepped next to Gareth. "We thought you would want to donate something like Lynne's dad, Mr. Stillwater and Mr. Thorn did." The expression on Winston's face challenged his dad to disagree.

Again Byron skimmed his gaze over everyone in the group, coming to rest on Maddy. A tic jerked in his cheek, and he narrowed his eyes on Gareth. "Time for you two to come home. The rocks can stay. Follow me in your truck." Then he stomped toward his vehicle.

The twins exchanged glances, then Winston mumbled to the group, "Sorry about that."

Heads down, they trudged to their pickup.

Ben jogged to them, and Winston rolled down the window. "Thanks for your help today and yesterday."

After the boys nodded, Gareth drove off, throwing a look at Maddy as he left.

Lucy took in a deep, calming breath. The twins had been wrong not to ask their father face-to-face, but her heart went out to the pair. Their relationship reminded her of what Ben had gone through with his dad. Byron had a strong personality that needed to dominate the people around him.

She shifted toward Maddy to see if she was all right

and glimpsed her swiping her hand across her cheeks. Christie had her arm around Maddy and was speaking to her in a low tone.

When Ben returned with deep lines of concern in his expression, he said, "This is a good start. Now all I have to do is come up with a maintenance plan for the garden. If any of you want to help, please let me know."

"There's a horticulture class at the high school. Maybe during the school year they might want to take this on as a project."

"Great suggestion, Rob. I'll talk with the teacher this week. The most important thing is the sign is back and looking good as people drive into Little Horn. Thanks for your help."

"Rob, I'll drive you home since Winston and Gareth had to leave," Christie said as she and Maddy headed for her Chevy.

When the teens left, Ben stood in front of Lucy, releasing a long breath. "That was tense."

"How are you?"

"I'm fine…" He shook his head and said, "That's not exactly right. It brought back memories of my own father and me, especially those last years in high school. Byron explodes at them, letting his anger go while those boys have to keep it buried inside them. It's like a pressure cooker. Something is going to give. I've been there with that kind of anger."

She'd had such a good childhood with supportive parents. Ben's situation, as well as the twins', reminded her that not all kids did. No wonder he wanted to work with young people. The more she was around him, the more she respected him. Ben could have turned out so different. "I'm going to leave before dawn tomorrow for

Lawton. I want to be back in time to arrest Gareth and Winston in the evening. I don't want to give them time to start robbing again."

"How about tonight?"

"I'm going to have a deputy keep an eye on their ranch. With that hill that overlooks Byron's property and his house, hopefully the deputy can alert me if the twins go anywhere."

"Now we just have to wait until tomorrow to see if the case is finally solved and Little Horn can return to normal." She was hopeful, but then she would no longer have any reason to spend time with Ben. And that thought bothered her more than it should have.

Chapter Ten

Hoping to find the lunch crowd gone, Ben parked near Maggie's Coffee Shop at one thirty on Monday and started to climb from his truck when his cell phone rang. He quickly answered when he saw it was Lucy calling.

"Good news?" he asked as he spied Byron leaving the restaurant.

"Yes, for the case, but not for the McKay family."

"So Gareth and Winston are the Robin Hoods. It makes sense knowing what's going on with them. When will you be back in Little Horn?"

"I'm on the road now. I'll probably be back in three hours."

"Would you be upset if I paid Byron a visit right before you come? I think his boys will need some support. I won't if you say no."

"What pretext are you going over to see him about?"

"Smooth over what happened yesterday."

"I can do this myself, but I agree about Gareth and Winston having some support if needed. This isn't going to be easy, but it will be nice to have an end to this case."

Ben watched the twins' father drive away. "And

maybe Byron will need it, too. I remember before you came yesterday that Winston mentioned his mother was visiting her sister in Houston for a few days."

"I didn't know that. I'll give you another call when I arrive in town. Talk to you later."

When Ben disconnected with Lucy, he didn't move from the front seat. He stared out the windshield, trying to figure out what was going on with him. With Lucy.

Although the situation wouldn't be a good one, he was looking forward to seeing her even briefly this evening. This wasn't like him.

A knock on his side window jerked him out of his thoughts, all centered on the sheriff. Ben nodded at Carson and finally climbed from his truck. "What are you doing in town?"

"Lucy called me to tell me what has developed in the Robin Hoods case. I understand she also told you."

"This is going to cause some problems in Little Horn."

Carson's laugh held no humor. "You think? We have our monthly meeting this week of the Lone Star Cowboy League. I'm scrapping my agenda. I'm sure the only thing the members will want to discuss will be what to do with Winston and Gareth. I want to make sure you're going to be there. You're not ready to lock the boys up and throw away the key like a good part of the town will want, especially with Byron's behavior about this situation. I can't even image Ruby's reaction. Positive her brother was the cattle rustler, Byron wanted to string up Derek when all this started."

"How are you going to break it to her?"

"Delicately." Carson pointed toward the restaurant. "Are you going inside?"

"Yeah, for a late lunch and because I need to see Abigail."

"Abigail? Is something going on? I've been in Austin a few days and everything falls apart around here."

"I'm going to see if Abigail is interested in being Cody's nanny."

"Don't let Maggie know."

Ben chuckled. "Are you going inside?"

"I wasn't, but I am now. I'm curious to see what Abigail says to the offer."

Ben made his way toward the coffee shop. "So do I. I'd better not hear any snickers coming from you."

The thinning lunch crowd allowed Ben to sit at a table in the back where he and Carson could have a quiet conversation and Maggie wouldn't hear him ask Abigail about the nanny position.

Abigail took their orders of chicken-fried steak, mashed potatoes and green beans, and Carson waited until she was out of earshot before asking, "When are you going to ask her?"

"Give me time. I have to think of the best intro. I want her to take the offer seriously and accept."

"Not take you seriously? Never."

"You mock me. Watch out. I might get my feelings hurt and be absent at the Lone Star Cowboy meeting. You'll have to deal with Byron all by yourself."

Carson tossed back his head and laughed. "Good thing we're such good friends or I would think you're serious."

"Oh, no. I'm never serious." Ben grinned, having missed this give-and-take with his childhood friend. If anyone knew what he'd gone through growing up, it was Carson, who had a difficult father, too. But his dad had come from love, whereas Ben wasn't so sure his father had loved him. "How's life with Ruby treating you? I go to sleep for a while and wake up to find you're a man in love."

After Abigail served them their lunches, Carson answered, "Ruby and I wasted so many years. We should have gotten married years ago, but my father never told me Ruby didn't accept the check he wrote to her to leave Little Horn without me."

Ben whistled. "Maybe what your father did tops mine."

"It isn't a contest, Ben. We both tried to please men who couldn't be pleased. I never thought I wanted to be a father, but with my nephew, Brandon, around, I've discovered I'm not such a bad dad. He's spending more time with my sister now, though, so I think by the start of school next fall she'll have full-time custody."

"And how do you feel about that?" Ben cut his chicken-fried steak and took a bite.

"I have mixed feelings. But my sister has a job she likes with the veterinarian. She really seems to be trying to be more responsible and a good mother when she's with Brandon. My nephew is responding to her, too. How about you and fatherhood?"

A well of emotions rose into his throat. Ben swallowed several times before answering. "I never thought I wanted to be a father, either, but Cody has changed my life in the past six weeks. I can't imagine not having him."

"Have you thought of finding a wife?"

After savoring some of his chicken-fried steak, Ben asked, "Why? Do you have anyone in mind?"

"I think you have someone in mind. Lucy."

"Those rumors going around about us are just that, rumors. We aren't really dating."

"Would you like to be?"

"Yes" was on the tip of Ben's tongue. Then he began thinking of all the reasons it wasn't a good option. "I need a mother for Cody. Lucy is married to her job and loves it."

"I'm not asking what Lucy wants. What do you want?"

"I don't know."

Carson sipped his water, assessing Ben over the rim of his glass. "That's a first. In the past you would have quickly answered, 'Having fun with no ties to anyone.'"

"That's the past. I have a son now that I have to consider." What if his interest in Lucy had more to do with Cody needing a mother than his falling in love? When he did commit to someone or something—like the ranch—it was totally. His family had fallen apart when his mother left them. He never wanted that for his son.

Ben looked beyond Carson and signaled for Abigail as she finished up with a customer.

When she approached, she placed their bills on the table. "Did you need anything else?"

Ben took a gulp of his ice water and asked, "You do a wonderful job with Cody in the church nursery. Would you consider working full-time as a nanny for Cody?"

Stunned, Abigail stared at him, opened her mouth, then snapped it closed.

Ben pushed a chair out for her to sit.

When the waitress sank into it, she finally said, "I don't know what to say. I never thought about doing that."

After Ben stated what he expected of a nanny and

how much he would pay her, he waited as Abigail processed the information.

Finally she panned the coffee shop, then said, "I need some time to think about it."

Ben removed his business card and scribbled his cell phone number on the back. "Call me."

She pocketed the card and rose. "I'll let you know by the end of the week." Then she scurried across the restaurant and disappeared into the kitchen.

"I've rarely seen Abigail speechless. She'd be a good choice as a nanny. She's worked at the church nursery since she was a teenager." Carson placed his money on top of his bill. "I need to be heading home."

"So do I." Ben followed suit, paying for his lunch, then standing.

As Ben drove in the direction of Stillwater Ranch, he thought of his son being held by a woman, and it wasn't Abigail. He remembered Lucy on Saturday rocking Cody because he was fussy when he woke up early from his nap. The peaceful look on her face had snatched Ben's breath.

With a warrant tucked into her pocket, Lucy pulled up to Byron McKay's huge mansion and parked behind Ben's truck. She had several deputies on standby in case Byron became difficult, but she wanted to keep this as low-key as possible. She knew the next hour or two would be rough, but seeing Ben's vehicle eased some of the tension gripping her.

On the porch, she rang the bell, then glanced around her at the sun setting, brilliant oranges and reds streaking across the blue sky. Beautiful. She wished she had time to appreciate it.

When the door swung open, Byron seemed to fill the whole entrance. A scowl darkened his features as he took in her uniform and the sheriff's SUV behind her, then her expression. "Is something wrong? Has there been another robbery?"

"No, I'm here to talk to your sons. I have some questions concerning the thefts and gifts."

"What in the world would Gareth and Winston know about them?" Byron's voice rose several decibels.

"I'd like all of us to sit down and talk. We can do it here or at the sheriff's office." Lucy peeked over the man's shoulder and spied Ben at the entrance to the living room and the twins on the second-floor landing, staring down at them.

"Are you arresting them? You're crazy if you think they would steal from me. Now I know we need a new sheriff." Byron remained in the doorway.

She'd had enough of his bluster. Straightening, she looked him in the eye. "You have a choice. We get to the bottom of this here or at my office. If they don't have anything to do with it, then no one else needs to know."

Byron gestured toward Ben. "He'll know."

Ben moved toward Byron. "I don't spread rumors. If Gareth and Winston are innocent as you say, then that is it."

Byron glanced from Lucy to Ben before snagging his sons' attention. "Come down here. I want this taken care of now and never brought up again. And, Ben, you stay. I want you to know the truth, too. My sons would never steal, especially from me. They have everything they want. Why would they need to?"

Gareth and Winston descended the staircase. A gray

tinge colored Gareth's face while Winston's expression was neutral.

Too bad the twins were under eighteen. She would love to talk to them without their father.

When they were settled in the living room with Ben standing by the entrance, Lucy sat in a chair across from the couch where Gareth and Winston were. Byron hovered at the end of the sofa, opening and closing his hands.

"Gareth, where did you get the money to purchase a silver music box, necklace and iPod?" Lucy thought she would start with the gifts to Maddy.

Gareth didn't reply for a long moment until Byron snorted and said, "What's that got to do with the cattle rustling? If you don't have more than that, leave."

"Gareth?" Lucy ignored Byron and kept her focus on the twins.

"Dad bought me my iPod, and I don't have a music box or necklace," Gareth finally mumbled, his gaze lowering.

"This is ridiculous—"

Lucy cut off Byron, saying, "I know you purchased the music box and necklace at a jewelry store in Austin."

Gareth hunched his shoulders.

"Even if he did, it has nothing to do with the case." Byron stepped closer to Gareth, and the sixteen-year-old stiffened.

Although she didn't see Ben, Lucy was aware of his presence. "When the Derrings received special presents at Christmas, Maddy also did and continued to after that. At that time it appeared the gifts came from the Robin Hoods. That was the consensus and why the robbers were given the name of Robin Hood. I started trying to find where the gifts were coming from."

"This still doesn't explain why my boys would do something like that. Steal from the rich to give to the poor? No way."

"But the piece of evidence that clearly identifies your sons as the thieves is Mark Ballard."

"Mark Ballard? Who is he?" Byron's voice lowered to a menacing hiss by the last question.

Winston dropped his head, twisting his hands in his lap.

"They sold cattle to him over months. He works out of Oklahoma and was brought in for selling stolen cows. He ID'd Gareth's and Winston's photos as someone he dealt with handling cattle and equipment they brought him."

"You're falsifying evidence. You're mad at me because I'm going to make sure you aren't the sheriff next year. In fact, when I'm through with you, you won't be next month. Where's the motive?"

"Your sons are upset at how Betsy and Mac McKay were treated last year. They needed help, and you wouldn't give them any. Mac's drinking led to his death, and Betsy left town months before she graduated from high school because of what happened. They were family, and you turned them away." Lucy directed her gaze to Gareth, who stared at her. "Isn't that right, Gareth? You and your brother were close to them."

"Mac was the cause of his own problems. He—"

With tears streaming down his cheeks, Gareth surged to his feet and glared at his father. "You are the reason he died. He had someone steal his cattle and some equipment and you wouldn't help him. He was more a father to me than you were. He always asked how we were doing. He listened to us when we had a problem. He'd try to help us." Gareth's face grew redder as he shouted. "Betsy is our cousin, and you let her leave town. You wouldn't even help her when her father died. You're a mean man, and I hate you."

Gareth rushed from the room and slammed out the front door.

Ben turned, heading after the teen. "I'll go get him."

Byron looked at Ben leaving and moved his mouth up and down, but no words came out of him. Lucy had never seen Byron so stunned or speechless.

He sank onto the couch next to Winston, his son's head still down. "Is that why you did it?" Byron finally asked the remaining twin.

Winston's Adam's apple bobbed up and down.

"Is it?" Byron said in a more demanding voice.

"Yes. There were a lot of people around here that needed help. You've got everything you need. They didn't. Mac was family."

Byron's gaze fell on Lucy. "I'm calling my lawyer. Not another word."

She nodded, then talked on her cell phone to one of the deputies waiting for her call. "We're ready."

When she disconnected, Winston looked at her with a pale face and huge eyes. "Ready for what?" His voice shook as he continued to twist his hands together.

"I have a warrant to search the ranch."

"But the cattle are gone."

"It still has to be done."

"Winston, I said not another word," Byron said as he reentered the living room.

"She's got a warrant to search the ranch."

Lucy withdrew the piece of paper and offered it to Byron.

He snatched it from her hand and scanned it. Rage mottled his face. "You'll regret this."

"Regret doing my job? I don't think the other ranchers will feel that way." She'd tried to make it as easy as possible for the twins' sakes, but Byron was determined to go down fighting. When she got to the sheriff's office, she would call Pastor Mathers. Maybe he would be able to give Byron the peace and guidance he needed.

Ben spied a dark figure disappear into the McKay's barn and hurried his pace. He could remember having that kind of anger buried deep inside him at Gareth's age. He should have been able to turn to Grady, but for some reason they'd pulled further apart. If he had had someone to talk to, maybe he wouldn't have chosen the reckless path he had. Instead, he'd kept it bottled up inside him and rebelled any way he could. He understood where the twins were coming from and hoped he could reach Gareth before he did something else destructive.

When Ben entered the dimly lit barn, he paused to see if he could hear any movement. Other than the rustling of a horse in a stall to his left, it was quiet. "Gareth, running from your problem won't change your situation. I'd like to talk to you. I've been where you are—angry with your father, wanting to lash out. Please let me help you."

A door opened to the tack room to the right and Gareth stood in the entrance. "No one can help me."

"I can listen to what you have to say. I'm discovering the more I talk about what's going on inside me the more I'm beginning to understand myself and my motives."

"You didn't steal from others."

"No, but I was wild. All I wanted for a while was just to have a good time, which meant drinking and being with women." Ben slowly covered the distance between them. "You know, I really wasn't having that much fun because so many times it was useless and meaningless. I just knew it would make my dad angry."

"What changed? Your dad dying?"

Ben shook his head. "No, I still did it after he died because I was still angry at him. But slowly as I became involved in running my ranch I began to replace that destructive behavior with something that had purpose. Ultimately my accident last year is what was the final epiphany for me. I woke up to discover I was responsible for my own son. I want to be the best example of a dad I can be. I don't want what happened between me and my father to happen between Cody and me."

"All my dad wants is his way. He doesn't care what Winston and me want or think. When we came home yesterday from helping to put up the sign, Dad yelled at us for half an hour, then ended with telling me I was not to see Maddy. She wasn't the type of girlfriend for a McKay. Now she's gonna hate me for what I did."

"I can't answer for what Maddy will do, but I know she cares about you."

"We're going to jail, aren't we?"

"You'll be arrested. What comes after that is up to the court. But running away won't change the situation, only make it worse. Face what you did and learn from it. I'll be here for you."

Gareth inhaled a deep breath, then exhaled it slowly.

"Are you ready to go back to your house?"

Gareth trudged toward the exit. "You really mean what you said? You'll be here for me?"

"Yes, and Winston. Y'all aren't alone." In that moment Ben realized he'd never been alone because the Lord was always with him. He also had Mamie, Cody and Grady…and now Lucy. But would she still be there now that the case was over?

Chapter Eleven

As she glimpsed Ben heading for her table at Maggie's Coffee Shop Wednesday evening, Lucy smiled. The gesture seemed alien, since the past two days all she'd been dealing with was the Robin Hoods case and the fallout from arresting Winston and Gareth. She didn't look forward to the meeting tonight of the Lone Star Cowboy League. Carson wanted her there to let the members know what was going on with the case. A lot of rumors were flying around town and tempers were high.

Abigail stopped Ben and said something to him. When he resumed his trek toward her, a frown furrowed his forehead.

"What's wrong?" she asked as he sat next to her.

"I asked Abigail to be Cody's nanny. She just told me no. After thinking about it and praying, she decided no. She likes her job here and doesn't see herself as a full-time nanny."

"I'm sorry to hear that. She would be good. You'll find someone. In the meantime, you'll have Chloe and Maddy to help. That gives you some more time to find the perfect solution."

After Abigail took their dinner orders, Lucy checked her watch. An hour, and then no telling what would happen.

"You're thinking about the meeting tonight."

"It's that obvious?"

He touched her forehead with his fingers, running them back and forth as though that would erase the lines and stress of the past months. "Byron has been pretty silent in the past twenty-four hours."

"Maybe Pastor Mathers's visit helped him."

"I'm not sure I see him changing anytime soon."

But from what she had seen, Ben had—or was the transformation temporary? "Why do you say that?"

"I went to see Gareth and Winston this morning, and Byron refused to let me talk to them. When I left, I glanced up at the second floor and saw one of the twins standing at the window. I believe Gareth, but I'm not sure. He's hurting, and he needs someone to talk to."

"Pastor Mathers?" With tempers flared, Ben was a voice of reason, and she appreciated that with all she was dealing with.

"I hope Byron will let him talk to the boys. I went to see our pastor before coming here. He's going to be at the meeting tonight, too."

"A calm voice in the midst of the angry ones."

"I pray people will listen."

Abigail set their dinners in front of them along with their bill. "I understand some people who aren't members are going to the meeting tonight."

Lucy nodded. "Carson opened it up to the public, but members and myself are the only ones allowed to talk." She slid a glance at Ben. "And perhaps Pastor Mathers."

"I have to work or I'd be there. Not sure many people

will be here tonight. But in the past couple of days that's all anyone is talking about. They can't believe Gareth and Winston stole the cattle and equipment, nor that they gave gifts to others."

When the waitress left, Ben frowned. "I think the boys care more for the townspeople than they realize. They could have sold the items and kept the money for themselves. They didn't. You said one of your deputies found a duffel bag with a lot of money in it, right? And a note addressed to Betsy said the money was rightly hers and that it came from Byron McKay's ranch."

"It still doesn't make it right."

"I didn't say it was. I'm just trying to look at it from all angles."

"This from the guy who used to think things were either black or white."

Ben picked up a piece of fried chicken. "I'm discovering nothing in life is that clear."

"But the law is."

"Not really, because judges and juries are human and don't always see it as clear-cut as the law is stated." He pointed to her chef salad. "You can have some of my fried chicken if that doesn't fill you up."

She laughed. "At the rate you're going you're going to be back to your preaccident weight. Then you won't get to flaunt all the high-calorie food in front of me."

"Even before the accident, I could pretty much eat what I wanted."

She harrumphed. "Your color has come back, too."

"Working more outside at the ranch. Spring is my favorite time of year."

"Mine, too."

"Ah, I knew we would eventually have something in common."

"We do besides that. We both care about Little Horn and the people." That was one of Ben's most endearing qualities. "Are you going to speak tonight?"

"Maybe. We'll see how it goes. What are you going to recommend?"

"I'm still waffling, but what you've said makes sense. Ultimately it will be the judge and DA, though, who make the decision."

"Not a jury?"

"I do want them to be tried as juveniles. I want to see them have counseling as part of their sentence."

"Because you don't think Byron would take them to a counselor?"

"I don't know, but I do know they need to have guidance and ways to handle their anger." Lucy stabbed her fork into her salad, her stomach churning at the thought of the evening before her.

"Carson started to cancel the Lone Star Cowboy meeting tonight. He wanted to give the town some time to process what happened. I talked him out of it."

Lucy lifted her palm to his forehead to feel his skin. "Has the hot sun baked your brain?"

"Not talking it over in a place where there is some kind of order and decorum doesn't mean feelings will go away. Like Gareth's and Winston's anger at their father, it will fester until someone explodes."

She studied his handsome face. "How did you get to be so wise?"

"When I was lying in the hospital bed after I woke up, I had a lot of time to think about life. I started thinking about the kind of world I want my son to grow up in.

I grew up with a lot of anger in me, but also there was anger in my father. I know I don't want that for Cody."

She prayed this Ben stayed around, but she'd seen many people profess to have changed and not, especially in her line of work.

Wall-to-wall people crammed into the meeting hall of the Lone Star Cowboy League's Little Horn chapter. Ben stood in the rear with Lucy, so near he could feel the tension pouring off her as heated conversations filled the room. She constantly scanned the crowd while two of her deputies stationed in other strategic places did the same.

As Carson called the meeting to order and ran through a few items, restlessness took hold of many surrounding Ben. Carson repeatedly called for order before he finally brought up the topic all the people were waiting for.

Ben leaned close to Lucy and whispered, "If you need any help, just say the word. I feel any second a war will erupt."

"Exactly. I should have had some of my off-duty deputies here, too."

"Did you noticed the ranchers stolen from are sitting on one side of the room while the ones who received gifts on the other?"

"Yep. With a big red line down the middle."

Ben clasped Lucy's hand near him while Carson said, "For the past six months we've been dealing with thefts of animals and equipment. It has caused numerous problems in this community. I have invited Sheriff Benson here to explain about the apprehension of the thieves and what will be done with the suspects. She is the only one who will talk right now, so remember that."

Lucy squeezed Ben's hand, then released it and strode

toward the front of the room. She walked with authority and assurance, as though she'd been the sheriff for a long time. The more he was with her the more he realized she was an incredible woman.

Lucy took the microphone that Carson handed her and paused while she took in the townspeople all staring at her. The silence in the hall hung for a long moment before she said, "On Monday night I arrested Gareth and Winston McKay for cattle rustling and robbery. Charges will be filed in juvenile court tomorrow morning, and they will go before Judge Nelson."

Some in the crowd jumped to their feet. "Juvenile court! They'll get a slap on the wrist and be back out in no time to terrorize us," Paul Martelli, one of the prosperous ranchers stolen from, shouted from the left side of the room.

Ben observed Byron seated next to Carson give the man a withering look, but that didn't stop another rancher who'd been hit to jump to his feet. "We need to make a statement that cattle rustlers are *not* tolerated here."

Dan Culter rose. "Yeah, I was robbed. I have enough to worry about."

Carson struck his gavel against the table several times but more joined in, some of the ranchers who benefited from the gifts trying to calm the irate ones.

Mr. Donner, one of the struggling ranchers, put his hand between his lips and blew a loud whistle. "I believe the sheriff has the floor, so sit down, act like the gentlemen you're supposed to be and listen."

A few grumbled, but the room grew quiet.

"One of the stipulations the DA is asking for is restitution for the ones robbed. The gifts I have confiscated will be sold, and the money will go into the fund. The method of raising the rest of the money needed will be decided by the court. We will need everyone affected to fill out a report of what was stolen and the value." Lucy went on to go over what had led to the arrest. "We are a community who has cared for our own for years. Don't let this cause a rift among you." She passed the microphone back to Carson, then moved off to the side but stayed in front.

Pastor Mathers walked down the middle aisle and said to Carson, "May I speak?"

Carson nodded.

The pastor, without the benefit of the microphone, swung around and faced the audience. "I'm not going to give a sermon tonight, but I'm going to challenge each one of you to forgive the McKay twins. That is what our Lord wants. That doesn't mean they won't be held accountable for their actions, but that isn't in your hands. The court will decide. But you can decide to show the teenagers grace. Only you."

Then the pastor retraced his steps and stood by the door in the back as though he was in church and going to greet everyone as they left.

Mr. Wentworth called out, "Byron, why haven't you spoken? You certainly had enough to say these past months about the case. Everyone has heard it."

"Yeah, more than once," Derek Donovan, one of the guys accused unjustly of being the thief, added when Mr. Wentworth sat down.

Byron yanked the microphone from Carson's hand and surged to his feet, his large bulk towering over everyone on the small stage at the front where the board sat. He panned the audience, his glare intimidating. "You have convicted my sons without the benefit of a trial. They have not been found guilty yet." His face reddened as he spat out the last sentence.

Worried the man might have a heart attack, Ben pushed off the back wall, his breath held.

Byron opened his mouth but the sound of a cell phone ringing from his pocket cut into rumblings rippling through the crowd. He retrieved the phone, turned away and answered it, speaking in a low voice.

All cell phones except the sheriff's were supposed to be silenced until the meeting was over, but it didn't surprise Ben that Byron didn't follow the rules. He thought he was outside them.

Suddenly Byron jerked to attention. The whole room heard him say, "Be right there." When he swung around, the color had been leeched from his face. He charged for the side exit near the stage.

Lucy stepped in his path and said something to Byron. Ben hurried toward them. Something was wrong. By the time he reached Lucy, Byron had slammed out of the room.

"What happened?" Ben asked Lucy.

"Gareth overdosed on sleeping pills. At least that's what Byron's wife said. His son has been taken to the hospital."

"Let's go. They need help." From Byron's performance and continual denial of what his sons had done, it was obvious he wasn't dealing with the situation, which probably meant the boys weren't, either.

"I'll tell Carson. Let Pastor Mathers know and meet me at my SUV."

Although others wanted to know what was going on, Ben made a beeline for the pastor, told him and quickly left before he was detained. He'd feared something bad would happen because the McKays were a dysfunctional family, much like what he'd had as a teenager.

It took Lucy five minutes to get to the hospital. When they arrived, Ben hopped out before she even turned off the engine and headed for the sliding glass doors of the small emergency room. He should have said more to Gareth. Maybe this wouldn't have happened.

Byron stood outside a room, gesturing and talking in a loud voice. "How long will that take?"

The doctor answered in a low tone so Ben couldn't hear what was said.

"He'll be all right after you pump his stomach?" Byron was in the man's face as though that would heal Gareth.

Lucy joined Ben, and they approached Byron as the ER doctor said, surprisingly patient, "Your wife is in there. She requested you stay outside. The room is small. I'll keep you informed."

"You tell Eleanor to come out here and explain to me why I have to stay out here."

The doctor entered the room and closed the door.

Byron started forward. Both Ben and Lucy hurried toward the man. Byron had made a scene over lesser issues. Ben stood in the man's path while Lucy grasped his arm.

"Byron, give the doctor time to work on Gareth. Can you tell me what happened?" Lucy's voice held such a soothing tone that Byron actually stopped and looked at her.

"What are you doing here? This isn't any of your business. Haven't you done enough?" Byron shook her hand off his arm. "You've made a mistake. My sons didn't do anything they said they did. They wouldn't steal from me."

Ben took a step toward the man. "We're only trying to help. I know you're upset and angry—"

"You don't know what I'm feeling. Did you hear my so-called friends talking about throwing the books at my sons?"

"What did you want them to do?" Ben asked, moving even closer to Byron.

"Give me time to fix this. My sons didn't know what they were saying. They are mad at me because of Mac."

Lucy came up beside Ben. "Besides the fact Gareth and Winston admitted what they did, there are other pieces of evidence, some found on your property during the search. There was a duffel bag with a letter to Betsy, telling her the money in it was for her."

Byron's gaze drilled into Lucy. "I'm going to challenge the search in court."

"Don't forget about Mark Ballard. He ties the boys to the cattle rustling."

"In order to get a better deal, he is accusing them. My lawyer can challenge that, too."

Ben glanced around and noticed people watching them. "Let's go where it's more private."

"They need to know my sons are innocent," Byron yelled.

Ben caught sight of Winston standing in the entrance to the waiting room. Myriad emotions flittered across the teen's face from surprise to anger to embarrassment. Ben headed to the sixteen-year-old, hoping that Byron would follow once he saw his son. "Let's go in here, Winston."

"Why's he here making a scene? He's the reason all

this is happening. Gareth could be dying. I couldn't wake him up. I..." Tears shone in the boy's eyes as he glanced toward the room where the doctor was treating his twin. He whirled around and ducked back into the empty waiting area.

Ben entered right behind the teen.

Wet tracks ran down the teen's face, and he scrubbed his knuckles across his cheeks. "Everything has to be his way no matter what. Well, guess what? This won't be. We're glad everyone knows, and *he* can't change the fact we're guilty. That's eating him up."

"Quit saying you've done it," Byron bellowed from the doorway.

Winston's eyes narrowed on his father. "No, I'm not. It's the truth."

"I don't have sons that are criminals. I—"

Winston charged his father. "Listen to yourself. It's always about you. I this. I that. Do you ever care what Gareth and me think or want?"

Byron started toward his son.

Ben quickly stepped between father and son. "This is not the time or place for this conversation." Ben stared into the large man's eyes until he finally backed into the hallway.

Byron glanced around, red invading his face, not from anger but embarrassment. He started to say something, but didn't. Instead, he strode toward the exit to the building.

"I'll go after him," Ben said to Lucy, then in a low voice added, "Winston is hurting. Stay with him."

"I will. Pastor Mathers went into the room where Gareth is." She took hold of his arm and for a few seconds peered at him. "Thanks for being here. This is a mess."

"I'll see what I can do for Byron, but I never could talk to my dad."

"You're not the same person."

Lucy's words stayed with him as Ben hurried outside to find Byron. The crisp air felt good as he panned the parking lot looking for Byron's truck. That was when Ben saw the man pacing by his vehicle, the security light illuminating him.

God, I need You to tell me what to say. I can't do this without You. Ben leaned on Byron's pickup, giving the man a chance to walk off some of his anger.

Finally Byron halted in front of Ben. "Have you come to gloat?"

"No. There's nothing to gloat about. I hope I can help you."

"Help me? Why? What do you want from me?"

"Nothing. I'm here for you."

Byron scowled, his eyebrows slashing down. "No one is here for me. All people ever want is something from me. Usually money. Don't get me wrong. I like being wealthy and have worked hard for my money. But I'm not an ATM."

"With wealth comes responsibility to the people around you."

"My daddy told me to be careful with my money or people will suck me dry. I'm just trying to show my boys the same way my father showed me."

"By being the town bully, trying to strong-arm everyone to do it your way."

Byron sucked in a deep breath. "You have no right—"

"I'm only pointing out what is happening. You think

by denying the truth about Gareth and Winston it will go away. That the townspeople will let them walk and you can go back to the same way things have always been."

Byron's mouth dropped open, his eyes round. "No one has ever dared say that to me."

Ben pushed himself off the back fender. "Then, it's time. In recent months I have had to face my past... shortcomings. Maybe it's time for you, too."

"I can't accept my sons are criminals. I brought them up better than that."

"You can continue to spout off that your boys are innocent, but they have stepped up and admitted their guilt. Winston told me earlier he and Gareth are glad they did. If your sons are ready to face the consequences of their actions, don't you think you should be there to support them rather than embarrass them?"

"Embarrass them? I'm trying to save them from themselves."

"Is the point to save them so they think they can get away with anything? That your money will buy them out of trouble? What kind of example is that?"

His eyes piercing Ben, Byron curled his hand into a fist.

"Go ahead. Hit me if you want. But I warn you, I'll strike back." Ben noticed Pastor Mathers approaching. "Quit thinking about yourself and think about your family. When you grow old and look back on your life, what will you have to show for yourself? Sons who want nothing to do with you? People who are scared of you? That's how my father died. Lonely and unhappy. He couldn't take his money with him, and neither can you."

Pastor Mathers joined them. "Good evening. Ben,

Lucy is inside waiting for you. She'll drive you back to your truck."

"Thanks," Ben murmured, hoping his words helped Byron deal with the truth. Unlike his father, his wasn't physical but emotional. It appeared Byron raised his sons as he had been raised. That made Ben even more determined to be a good example for Cody.

As he started for the entrance, Ben overheard the pastor saying, "Byron, I came to tell you Gareth is being moved to a room for overnight observation. He's in transient right now but will be in room 124. I thought you and I could pray for his recovery."

The sight of Lucy at the emergency room sliding doors lifted Ben's spirits after the intense few hours.

She smiled. "I was afraid I would find you two battling it out."

"We were, with words. Are you able to leave?" A strong urge to hold his son inundated Ben.

"Yes, I'm coming back tomorrow morning, not as the sheriff but a friend. Gareth will be evaluated before he leaves the hospital." Lucy strolled toward the sheriff's SUV.

Inside her vehicle Ben sighed, exhaustion suddenly blanketing him. "I feel as though I've worked for the past twenty-four hours."

"I'm praying for peace for Little Horn." Lucy left the hospital parking lot.

"And that people can put this behind them, especially at the Easter-egg hunt this weekend."

"What time do you need me on Saturday?"

"Eight. I'll have a mug of Mamie's coffee waiting for you."

"Ah, what an incentive for me, but do you think that's

early enough? The hunt starts at ten and a lot of kids show up early." She pulled up to the side of his truck and angled toward him. "Thanks for all your help with the twins. I think that outburst in the waiting room actually helped Winston."

"What about their arraignment tomorrow morning? There's no way Gareth will be strong enough to be there."

"I talked with Eleanor, and she's going to call their lawyer and ask for it to be postponed until Friday. I can't imagine the DA not agreeing, but I'll be at his office first thing in the morning to make sure."

In the dim shadows of her vehicle, Ben wanted to pull her across the seat and kiss her. Instead, he gazed at her as though this was the first time he'd really seen her. She cared for this town and its people. She was the right person to be the sheriff.

When he didn't move to leave, she asked, "Is there something else?"

"Yes."

He took her hand and gently tugged her toward him, his fingers delving into her hair to cup the back of her head. His lips grazed hers once, twice before settling on hers and surrendering to the sweetness of the kiss. When she pulled back, their gazes linked across the small space between them.

"See you Saturday," Ben said in a thick voice, then slipped from the front seat and paused as Lucy drove away. After the Easter-egg hunt there wouldn't be any reason for them to see each other. His shoulders sagged at the thought. Somehow he would have to put Lucy out of his mind in the months to come and concentrate on Cody and finding a good nanny for him.

Chapter Twelve

Lucy reached to ring the doorbell at the Stillwater Ranch, but the door swung open before she had a chance. Ben stood in the entry with a mug in his hand, steam wafting upward.

"I just poured this for you." He pushed open the screen to let her inside and passed her coffee to her, then retrieved his on the hallway table.

"I noticed the tent has been set up."

"Zed, Grady and I did it yesterday afternoon and set up the tables and chairs for the arts-and-crafts station. I figured since it wasn't supposed to be windy we could get that done beforehand and give ourselves a few minutes to enjoy our coffee. Did you have any breakfast?"

"I got up later than I planned."

He smiled and took her hand, starting for the back part of the house. "Good. Grandma is making one last batch of Texas-size French toast, and I haven't had a chance to eat, either. I was up late with Cody, and if Mamie hadn't awakened me this morning, I might not be up now. My son gets to sleep in."

"I'm jealous. Why was he up late last night? His tooth?"

As Ben entered the kitchen, he shrugged. "I don't know. He has that tooth, and I don't see any others coming in. Maybe it was because he had a long nap later than usual yesterday. At the Easter-egg hunt, I'm going to wear him out so he takes one on time today."

Listening to Ben, Lucy realized how well suited the role of dad was to him. When he talked about his son, he beamed. He was a natural like her father. "I've got some good news. Dad and Mom are coming home this week for a month before heading back out on the road."

"That's great. I know you've been wanting them to for some time."

"Normally I don't like surprises, but when they called last night, I loved hearing that."

"When was the last time they came?"

"Christmas, but only for a short time, then they headed for Florida and warmer weather. I never thought of my parents as snowbirds." The scent of fried bacon, coffee and French toast stirred her appetite.

"What's this about snowbirds?" Mamie asked as she took the French toast out of the pan and brought it to the table.

"My parents. I was telling Ben they are coming home next Tuesday."

"It'll be nice to see your parents again. You need to bring them out to the ranch one evening for dinner. How about Thursday?" Mamie walked back to the counter and picked up a platter of bacon and set it in the middle of the table.

"They'll enjoy it. They always do when they come out here. Mom raves about your cooking." Lucy sprinkled powdered sugar over her French toast.

"Where are Grady and Chloe?" Ben asked, then took

a bite of his thick French toast dripping in maple syrup and butter.

"Already down at the barn setting up the race area." Mamie headed for the door. "I'm bringing Cody down to the egg hunt. I've heard him fussing around upstairs in his bed. And don't worry about the dishes. Martha Rose will be back soon to take care of them. She delivered some treats for the kids setting up this morning."

Even with only powdered sugar, the breakfast was delicious and the coffee perfect. "I could get spoiled eating here, or rather I'd probably add pounds in no time."

"Not with all you do. You're rarely in your office."

"I should wear one of those counters that keep track of your steps."

"Easily ten thousand steps for you."

"You're right. Pass me the maple syrup." She poured some on the last half of her French toast.

"We'd better hurry. This expanded Easter-egg hunt was my idea. I don't want my brother thinking I'm slacking on the job."

"How are you two doing?"

"Actually good. He enjoys the cattle management, and I like the training and handling of the horses. I'm wanting to expand where we raise broncos for the rodeo circuit. I think diversifying will be good for the ranch. When beef prices are down, hopefully the other areas we are in will be doing good."

"And you've got connections with the rodeo world." Lucy finished her last bite and washed it down with lukewarm coffee.

"Yeah. It's nice to have those years come in useful for the ranch."

"Do you miss riding in the rodeo?"

"No. It was fine for a few years, but my life is here. If it hadn't been for my precarious relationship with my father, I probably wouldn't have pursued the rodeo circuit in the first place. I have more than enough to keep me busy here." Ben shoved his chair back and rose. "Ready?"

"Yep, but I'm grabbing another cup of coffee to take with me."

Ben refilled her mug and his, then made his way toward the front entrance. The sound of Cody crying rang through the house. He glanced upstairs. "I know Grandma is with him, but something might be wrong. I'll be right back."

"Take your time if you need to. I'll go down to the barn and start working on the arts-and-crafts tent. I'll make sure your brother knows you are seeing to Cody, not twiddling your thumbs."

"It won't be long before he'll be in the same place."

Lucy left out the front door, paused on the large porch and took a deep breath, the air perfumed with the honeysuckle in the flower beds along the house. No doubt one of Mamie's touches. She descended the stairs and headed for the barn, a spring to her step. The Robin Hoods case was solved, and her county could get back to business as usual. She prayed Pastor Mathers's words Wednesday night would help heal the tension that the area had been under for six months.

As she neared the tent setup, she pushed the thought of work from her mind. Ben had it right. This was for the children and nothing was going to spoil it.

Until she entered the tent and saw Maddy with Christie, crying.

* * *

Ben rushed into Cody's room and found Grandma Mamie rocking him while he bawled. "What's wrong?"

"He felt hot, and I took his temperature. It's a hundred and one. He's stuffed up and has been rubbing his ears. I know Tyler and Eva are coming. I think Tyler should check him out. He might have an ear infection."

"I'll call him. What can I do?" Listening to Cody crying broke his heart and made him feel helpless.

"Nothing. You used to get them when you were young. If it's an ear infection, Tyler will write a prescription for him."

"But he has a fever."

"This won't be the last time he does. It's part of growing up. I gave him baby Tylenol."

"I'll take him while you call Tyler." He needed to hold his son, make sure that Cody knew he was here for him.

He took his son from his grandmother's arms, then sat in the rocking chair when she left to phone Tyler. Cody looked up at his face, tears in his eyes. The sight tore at Ben's composure. "Son, we're getting help for you."

Cody rubbed the left side of his head against Ben's shoulder, his crying easing into whimpers. Ben rocked him and hummed a new country-and-western tune he'd heard on the radio the other day. Slowly his son nodded off, and by the time Mamie had returned Ben had risen to put Cody to bed.

"I'm amazed at how he's taken to you." His grandmother peeked into the crib.

Ben moved to the hallway and said in a low voice, "When is Tyler coming?"

"He and Eva were already on their way. He has his

medical bag with him, so he'll come up to the house when they get here."

"Good. Let me know if I need to drive into town and get a prescription for Cody."

"Eva already said she would. You need to be at the barn. This is your shindig."

"But I shouldn't leave him."

"Why not? I raised your father, you and Grady. I think I can handle Cody. I looked out the window and everything is proceeding as planned but you know how that can change." She waved him away. "Go now. The kids will arrive in an hour and a half."

Ben hesitated.

"You aren't abandoning your child."

"I've got my cell with me. Call if Cody gets worse."

"I will."

He walked away slowly, not sure if he could immerse himself in the Easter-egg hunt when Cody wasn't feeling well. No one was better than Grandma when a child was sick. By the time he'd neared the tent, he'd convinced himself he was doing the right thing.

When he entered, the area was empty except for Maddy and Lucy, sitting at a table in the corner. The teenage girl's back was to him, but the look of concern on Lucy's face urged him forward.

"What's wrong?" he asked as he approached.

Maddy twisted about, her eyes red, but Lucy was the one to say, "Two of the girls made some catty remarks in front of Maddy about Gareth stealing to give her gifts."

"But he didn't. Gareth used his own money to buy those gifts. He told me when he called me."

"When did you talk to him?" Ben sat across from Lucy.

"This morning before I left the house to come here. He wanted me to tell you he's sorry about not being able to help today. His father won't let him."

Ben recalled Wednesday evening when the teen had overdosed on sleeping pills. "In this case with all that has happened this week, that's probably a good decision."

"That's what I told him. He needs to consider what's best for him. He didn't mean to take all those pills. He hadn't been able to sleep, and he kept taking them."

"What did you say to the girls?"

"That Gareth needed our prayers, not condemnation."

"I hope they listen." Hopefully time would heal the wounds the teenagers' actions had caused.

Lucy glanced toward the entrance into the tent. "Candace is here. We need to finish setting up. Maddy, can you have Christie and Lynne return to help?"

"Sure."

"I wonder if Byron knows that Gareth is calling Maddy," Ben murmured as the girl left.

"Yes, he does. In fact, she is going to dinner at his house after church tomorrow."

"She is? Byron agreed to that?"

"According to Gareth, he suggested it. She's a bit intimidated by the invitation, but she wants to support Gareth. She has a gift. She looks at the best in everyone."

"We need more like her in Little Horn."

Grady stuck his head into the tent. "Since Gareth and Winston aren't coming, I need some help with the races. I've mowed the field, but there are some holes we need to fill in. I don't want a kid breaking his leg."

"I'm coming." Ben looked back at Lucy, said, "I'll see you around," then winked at her.

* * *

Over two hundred children ran around looking for Easter eggs in three separate areas. In the barn, the babies to three-year-olds were in a special place to look for their treats, with Chloe and Amelia supervising. Lucy watched over the four- to seven-year-olds while she spied Ben and Grady with the kids eight to twelve.

"Remember, when your basket is full, you need to stop hunting for the eggs," Lucy called out in the front yard as she walked around seeing where any hidden goodies still were, then helping the youngest to find them.

Eva joined her. "Sorry I was late. I had to run to town for a prescription for Cody."

"He's sick?"

"Ben didn't tell you? He has an ear infection."

"No, but we've only seen each other from afar, except when he first came out. Maddy was having a problem, and we dealt with that. Then everything got crazy." Lucy studied Eva a few seconds. When she saw Tyler and Eva together, she was reminded what a good marriage was like. Her parents had it. As a young girl, she'd yearned for one like theirs. "Something is different lately, Eva."

"Am I that obvious?"

Lucy nodded.

"I'm not sure if you've heard or not, but Tyler and I are looking into adopting a child. It will take a while, but the idea of having a baby thrills us."

Lucy hugged her friend. "I hadn't. That's great. You'll make a wonderful mother. I saw how good you were with Cody."

"I don't want too many people knowing since it's a long process."

"I'll pray for you two. You and Tyler will make good parents."

Eva beamed and shifted her attention to the young ones still hunting eggs. "The children are having so much fun."

"What I like is once they have a full basket they can go do something else with the other activities."

"Ben knows how to throw a party."

"Yes, he's good with kids." Lucy scanned the area for Ben. No wonder he'd looked troubled when he'd first come in the tent.

"Both Ben and Grady were always good to me when I followed them around growing up. Ben has a way with children."

"Will Cody be all right?"

"Yes. Maybe a little fussier than usual, but the medicine should work soon. It's handy to have a doctor around. We were on the way when Aunt Mamie called. Tyler always takes his medical bag with him, so we just kept coming."

"I guess that's why I haven't seen Mamie with Cody. I was hoping to hold him."

"Why don't you go relieve her for a while? I know she was looking forward to seeing the children."

"Are you okay by yourself?"

"You were. See all the moms and dads hanging around taking pictures? I'll recruit one of them if I need someone."

Lucy started for the house. "Where are they?"

"They're upstairs in Cody's room."

As she walked toward the house, Lucy smiled at the news from Eva. She hurried her pace because she wanted to hold Ben's son. When she did, she felt as if she'd come home. Probably not what she should feel, but the baby was so adorable and trusting. She could get lost in his big brown eyes with those long dark lashes. They reminded her of Cody's father. The vision of Ben with his son in her mind sped her heartbeat.

Inside, she mounted the staircase two at a time. When she entered his room, Mamie finished changing his diaper, then glanced back at her.

"He's been fed, had another short nap and his medicine seems to be working." Mamie picked Cody up and turned toward Lucy. "How's the egg hunt going?"

"The kids are having a great time."

"I'm glad. Ben was worried that y'all couldn't pull it off so quickly."

"May I hold him?" Lucy held out her arms, and Ben's grandmother passed the baby to her.

"Is that why you're here?" A twinkle brightened Mamie's eyes.

"Yes, he's adorable, but don't get any ideas. I actually came to let you go to the egg hunt for a while."

"Sure, Lucy. You keep telling yourself that. You'd be a terrific mom like your own."

"Ben and I are not dating. We've been spending time together because of the case and the Easter-egg hunt. That's all."

One of Mamie's eyebrows rose. "I won't be long. You'll be needed in the arts-and-crafts tent after refreshments are served." She strolled toward the hallway. "I appreciate your giving me a break. It'll be nice when everything is settled with a nanny or…" Her voice trailed off as she moved farther away.

Lucy held Cody out and in front of her. "Your great-grandma will have you fixed up with a girl before you know it, but if you're anything like your daddy, you'll run. So, big boy, what do you want to do?"

He flung his body from side to side.

"Are you telling me you want down?"

He gurgled and answered with gibberish.

"Okay." She scanned the room. "Let's go downstairs, where it looks like most of your toys are."

She cuddled Cody against her and headed for the stairs. His sweet baby scent stirred yearning in her heart.

Ben searched the kids swarming the refreshment table with various teenagers trying to keep order as they served the snacks and punch. Where was Lucy? In fifteen minutes the children would be ready to rotate through the different activity stations.

Then his gaze zeroed in on his grandmother. Who was with Cody? Was he asleep? He headed for Grandma. "How's Cody doing?"

"Great. Lucy relieved me for a while. I thought I would bring Cody outside to enjoy a few minutes of fun. I see you set up a little petting zoo for the young ones. When did you do that?"

"Last night I started thinking the babies and toddlers might not do the crafts or races, and I don't know how long they would listen to a story. But animals seem to enthrall them, so I had a few ranchers bring some and set up a small pen in the barn. Ruby brought a pony so a parent can walk around holding a young one on its back."

His grandmother looked him up and down. "Where was this side of Ben Stillwater hiding? That's a great suggestion to entertain the ones under two or three. Don't be surprised if you have some four- and five-year-olds in the pen, too."

"I'm going to get Cody. Are you staying?"

"Yes, this is where the action is."

Ben strolled toward the house. When he stepped inside the entry hall, he heard giggles coming from the living room. At the entrance he stopped and watched Lucy.

Her arms out in front of her, she said, "You can do it. You walked along the furniture like a pro. Grab my hand."

Cody smiled, scooted to the end of the couch and studied Lucy's fingers only a couple of feet away. His son took one step toward her. Then letting go of the cushion edge, he walked toward her until he realized he wasn't holding Lucy or the sofa. His eyes widened, and he plopped down on his bottom.

Lucy scooped him off the floor. "You did it, Cody. Two steps by yourself." She twirled him around, his giggles filling the air. Then Lucy saw Ben. Her face flushed, she brought Cody down next to her chest. "How long have you been there?"

"Long enough to see my son's first steps." Ben's heart swelled at the sight of Cody in Lucy's arms as though he belonged there.

"We were playing with his ball and he was so close to going and getting it once that I thought I'd encourage him."

"I can see in his eyes he wants to badly. I came up to get y'all. Mamie sent me. She wants Cody to see the petting pen."

"He'll love it. Where is she?"

"Near the arts-and-crafts tent." When she started to give him Cody, he shook his head. "He likes you holding him."

"And I like holding him."

As they made their way to the Easter-egg hunt, Cody played with Lucy's gold stud in her right ear, trying to figure out how it got there. Ben was ready to intervene if he pulled on her ear, but soon his fascination turned to all the children and adults at the ranch.

"He's so curious. Reminds me of you." Lucy looked sideways at Ben.

"Yeah, I got into a lot of trouble because of my curiosity."

"Are you going to be in the tent or at the field where the races are?"

"In here. Grady thought Chloe should help him in case a girl has a problem, but I'm not sure how much help I'll be. I never color within the lines."

"Whereas, I would get upset if I went out of the lines."

"And yet, you and I get along. Amazing."

Lucy stopped near Mamie, and she took Cody. "What's amazing?"

"My son. I saw him take a couple of steps by himself today."

Mamie grinned. "He did! He must have wanted something a lot."

Ben's eyes gleamed. "Yes, he did. Lucy."

"Ah, I see. Good taste, Cody," Mamie said to his son.

"Okay, you two, if you're trying to make me blush, you are succeeding. I'm going inside to see what Candace wants me to help with."

"I'll join, Lucy. I see a herd of kids coming this way."

For the next hour Ben was so busy going from one child to the next that when the Easter-egg hunt was over, he was surprised. He peered at Lucy across the room, the sunlight slanting in through the entry and pooling about her. She'd suggested several women for him to date who would make a good mother for Cody, but she was the one her son responded to. And he knew she did to his son. But that wasn't the main reason he'd rejected all those other women.

In that moment Ben realized he'd fallen in love with Lucy—at least this was what he thought the deep ache for her coupled with the need to be with her all the time was. In his twenty-eight years, he'd never allowed himself to care that much about a woman. He could say this had sneaked up on him, but not really. This past month had been surreal—flying by but at the same time crawling by. When he was with her, he couldn't believe how fast their time together passed, but then when he wasn't, all he thought about was seeing her again.

But where did he stand with her? Did she still think of him as the old Ben, never dating a woman for long? His gut tightened. He'd always been the one to walk away, not the other way around.

Later that evening Lucy finally plopped into a cushioned chair on the back porch at the Stillwater Ranch. "The dishes and kitchen are clean, and my legs hurt from being on my feet so much today. Where's Ben and Grady?"

Chloe sat in the lounger and propped her legs up. "At the barn, checking to make sure everything was returned to its former place. Ben forgot to take down the pen for petting animals, so he and Grady went to do it."

"Did Cody go down all right?"

"Yeah, and Mamie went to bed right after she put Cody in his crib. Today was a good one but tiring. My feet are swollen. Which has happened a few times since being pregnant." Chloe leaned back and sighed. "I may never move from this spot."

"I know what you mean, but I've got to drive home soon. I thought I would wait until Ben got back and say good-night to him." Lucy stared at her lap for a long moment, then asked, "Do you think Ben has changed since we were teenagers?"

"Yes, he's about two inches taller and twenty more pounds, all muscles. Well, he was before the coma, but his weight is returning. I've enjoyed working with him on his physical therapy. He didn't give me grief like Grady did at first."

"Grady's leg is so much better. He hardly limps anymore."

"That's because I insisted he do his therapy. Men can be so stubborn at times."

"I'm glad to hear Ben is cooperating with you."

"The old Ben might not have. He never took many things seriously. But he does now."

Yes, she'd noticed that, especially his son, but would it last? As a police officer she'd seen many people confess to be changed, but the first trouble they got into they reverted to their old ways.

"What's wrong?"

Lucy shook her head. "Just thinking back to when we were teenagers. I realized I had a crush on Ben in high school for a time, then he broke a friend's heart when he stopped dating her."

"Linda?"

"Yes. Within days he was dating another girl, who lasted about two months."

"And this is an issue, why?"

Lucy shrugged. "I care about him. In fact, my feelings concerning him scare me."

"You just care? That's all?"

"We're friends. Scratch that. We're more, but I can't go through another bad relationship. I thought I knew Jesse so well, and I didn't. Before we started seeing each other, Jesse had been a womanizer who convinced me he wasn't that person anymore."

"Like Ben?"

Lucy nodded. "How can I ever really trust him?"

"Good question, and I don't have an answer."

"How did you with Grady? Your ex was a cad."

"I prayed and turned it over to the Lord because I think it's impossible to know everything about a person. You have to decide what you want in life and how much you'll risk to have it."

Male voices coming from the kitchen drew Lucy's gaze to the window. "Grady and Ben are back."

"If you need to talk, I'm always here," Chloe said hurriedly as the back door opened and the men joined them. She glanced up at Grady and held her hand out. "You're just in time to help me up from this chair. I'm ready for bed. Mamie has the right idea."

Grady tugged Chloe to her feet. "Sounds good to me. Good night, Lucy, Ben."

Ben slipped in the chair beside Lucy. "Now I'm positive everything has been taken care of. Tomorrow will be a day of rest, one I need."

"I'm with you on that. This week has been long and difficult. But other than those two girls saying something to Maddy, I didn't hear anyone talking about Gareth and Winston. Did you?"

"No, but then children were around and some people

might get riled and cause a scene. So glad they didn't." Ben leaned his head against the back cushion and stared at the ceiling.

"I have only one more thing to do involving this case. Find Betsy. You said something about the Dallas/Fort Worth area."

"Yeah, the private detective I hired is running down some leads. He established she was there last fall, but she isn't in the apartment he had an address for."

"Next week I can try again to see what I can discover. I was spread so thin that I really didn't have the time to put much effort into the search. I'll feel better at least contacting her and making sure she's all right." She needed to go, but once she sat down she didn't want to get up; it was as though weariness glued her to the seat.

"I'll be talking with the private investigator in the next day or two, and when he's got a solid lead, I'm going to the Dallas/Fort Worth area and assist in the search. I won't feel right until this is resolved. We didn't do right by her. I'm hoping Betsy will come back to Little Horn."

"With Byron here? I'm not sure she will."

"Maybe Byron will learn from this and change. Maddy is going over there for dinner tomorrow after the Easter service. I never thought that would happen."

"Do you think he can change?"

"I don't know. Time will tell, but I think he got scared when Gareth took the sleeping pills. Maybe it'll be enough for Byron to see his high-handedness was driving his sons away from him."

"Yeah, but you know the old saying you can lead a horse to water, but you can't make him drink it."

"With anything, the motivation has to be there for it to truly work. We still need to go out and celebrate the case being solved. How about Monday night before your parents come into town?"

"A date?" She needed him to clarify what he thought this relationship between them was. Friends? More?

"It's time for us to admit what's going on between us isn't just being friends. At least for me." He scooted his chair around so he could see her and clasped her hands. "I love you, Lucy. When you were trying to fix me up with other ladies in town, no one interested me but you. You are who I need."

He loves me. Is it really love? Panic raced through her, and she tugged her hands free and rose, sidling away. "Do you know what love is? You spent most of your life avoiding it. Now you want a mother for Cody and you see how much I care about your son, but marriage is so much more than that."

He pushed to his feet. "I know marriage is."

"I worked hard to become sheriff, and I don't want to give it up." Lucy backed away. "I like helping the people of this county."

"I know how hard you work, and I haven't asked you to quit your job. I'm not even talking about marriage. I'm talking about loving you."

"I've always been here. Why now all of a sudden?" She wouldn't risk her heart again. Jesse had been a reformed playboy who talked a good game, then cheated on her. "This has come out of the blue." She spun around and started for the back door to grab her purse and leave before she gave in and believed he could change that much.

He followed.

She held up her hand. "I can let myself out. In fact, I prefer to."

After yanking the door open, she fled inside, relieved that he didn't come in with her. As she headed toward her Mustang, she realized she'd thrown every excuse at him but the one that frightened her enough to walk away from a man she was falling in love with when she knew she shouldn't. She wanted a total commitment from the man, and she didn't think Ben could change that much.

Chapter Thirteen

Ben sat at the kitchen table, sipping his coffee. He hadn't slept more than an hour last night after talking with Lucy. Maybe he deserved her rejection. How many times had he walked away when a woman started getting serious?

He lifted his mug in a toast. "Touché."

"Who are you talking to?" Grandma Mamie asked as she came into the kitchen and looked around. Her forehead's wrinkles deepened. "No one?" She picked up the coffeepot. "It's empty. How long have you been up?"

"A few hours. I finally got tired of staring at the ceiling in my bedroom and came down here."

Mamie shot him a quizzical look, then went to work preparing another pot full of coffee. While it was brewing, she moved to the table and sat across from Ben. "So what had you up all night? Lucy?"

"How did you know?"

"It's your hangdog look. What happened after I went to bed?"

"I told her I loved her, and she got out of here so fast you would think a wildfire was after her."

In spite of the seriousness, Mamie grinned. "That doesn't sound like our sheriff. I know she has feelings for you. Anyone who sees you two together sees it."

"Well, tell her that. She didn't get the memo."

"Tell me what you said and her reply."

As though he had the scene from the night before memorized, he repeated all the reasons she gave him that it wouldn't work between them.

Mamie held up her forefinger. "Number one, you did spend your youth running from any kind of commitment."

"Okay, I admit I did. I knew I wouldn't be a good husband, not while I held such anger toward Dad in my heart. But that doesn't mean I can't change my mind."

"Okay, let's say you've changed. How can she be sure?"

"Because I've never given my word and not meant it. When I dated those women, they knew up front I wasn't looking for a long-term relationship."

"Two, what about her job? How do you feel about a wife working?"

"That's why I'm looking for a nanny. I recognize we need help here with Cody, and Chloe's baby due in a couple of months. And I have already set up something for the summer."

"But Maddy will go back to school in the fall. I wish I could do it all," Mamie said with a sigh, "but I know my limits. I'm seventy-eight and don't have the energy I used to when you boys were growing up."

"I know. Lucy is good at her job. If she wants to work, I don't want to stand in her way. All that would cause would be resentment."

"Like your mother toward my son."

"Let's face it, that was why she left. She wanted more than being a mother and wife."

"Did you bother talking it out with Lucy? There are solutions. I helped raised y'all, and we could hire a good nanny for Cody and Chloe's child. It's not as if we wouldn't be around to make sure the nanny does a good job. What's nice about your job is you can be flexible. Lucy as sheriff wouldn't be able to as much as you. Her hours can be unconventional. That might be what concerns her. I think there's more to it, though, than her job."

"What?"

"Could it have to do with why she came back to town three years ago? I know from her mother she'd been dating someone seriously, then suddenly it was over and Lucy left the San Antonio Police Department."

"She told me about the guy she dated for a year. At the time they were talking marriage, he was seeing two other women."

Grandma Mamie pressed her lips together into a hard, thin line. "That can definitely make a person gun-shy. Did she tell you she didn't love you? Was that one of the reasons?"

Ben thought back to the conversation, remembering an almost scared expression on Lucy's face, and shook his head. "You're right. That might be it. Maybe it wouldn't work in the long run if she sees that other guy every time she sees me. Look at how long I've been dealing with my relationship with Dad. He influenced me a lot in my youth."

"He was an unhappy man that took his anger out on the ones he loved. It's not right, but unlike the McKay twins, who let their feelings toward their father cause them to make some bad decisions, we have to make the best of what's given to us. Talk to Lucy. What do you have to lose? You have a lot to gain if you love her."

"Thanks for helping me. You are a wise woman." Ben walked to the counter, refilled his mug and poured coffee for his grandmother, then returned to the table and gave it to her. "I'm going riding. I have some decisions to make and this is a good time to work some things out. It's quiet and nothing beats a sunrise around here."

Ben kissed Mamie's cheek, then left out the back door, nursing his coffee as he ambled toward the barn. He spied Thunder in a paddock close by, his black coat shining in the sun as the rays spread outward from the horizon. Pausing, he rotated slowly, taking in his ranch. What if he was wrong and he hadn't changed enough for Lucy? He only wanted to be married once.

Lucy hung up the phone after talking with the DA about the Robin Hoods case, pleased everyone was on board with the boys being tried in juvenile court. She liked Judge Nelson. He could be reasonable and creative. Gareth and Winston would pay for their crimes but at the same time get help. And she might not have considered the teenage boys' side of what had happened if it hadn't been for Ben.

When he'd said he loved her on Saturday night, she'd been stunned because she remembered once right after graduation Ben declaring he would never marry. It was too restrictive. He'd been adamant, citing what had happened to his parents' marriage. His mother had come back for graduation, then left immediately, and Lucy wondered if that was the reason for his statement.

That was ten years ago.

She'd changed in that time. Had Ben changed enough?

A movement in the main part of the sheriff's station drew her attention. Her dad was here and talking to the dispatcher. One of her deputies came in and joined their conversation.

Her parents had arrived the night before. And she needed their distraction, or all she would think about was Ben. The days since she had seen him at church on Easter had been the longest ones. She'd even caught herself earlier before her parents showed up wanting to call Ben or go out to see him at the Stillwater Ranch, but when she finally had called and Chloe answered, she'd discovered Ben had left that morning and would be gone all day. Chloe hadn't been sure when he would be coming back.

Was he leaving for good? She didn't think so because Little Horn had always been his home, but she couldn't shake the doubt completely away.

Her dad stuck his head through the opened doorway. "Ready to go to lunch at Maggie's? I sure miss her good food."

"Is Mom coming?"

"Nope, she's visiting with some friends, then stopping by Olivia Barlow's ranch. She was so happy to see Olivia has a man in her life now. You know how your mother frets over others in need, and Olivia certainly had been in need with her triplet boys."

"Clint Daniels will make a wonderful father for those boys." Lucy rose and headed out of the sheriff's station with her father. "I forgot to eat breakfast again, so I'm hungry."

"Good. Alice noticed that this morning and made me promise to make sure you ate a big lunch. I told her not to worry. You're doing just fine but that won't stop her. According to her, she won't stop worrying about you until she's dead."

"A mother's job is never done."

"And neither is a father's." Her dad pulled open the door to Maggie's and gestured for Lucy to go first.

After Abigail showed them to a table and took their orders, Lucy decided to approach the subject of the Robin Hoods case with her dad before he brought it up. "As I'm sure you know, the cattle rustlers were finally caught last week."

"Yes, a good job at tracking down the evidences."

"But it took me months to solve the case."

"That happens sometimes. Cattle rustlers can be hard to catch. Often they work in an area, then move on before they are caught. In the twins' case their robberies had to do with settling a score in their minds, not making money."

"I heard this morning Byron has started paying back the ranchers who the boys stole from. Carson came by the station this morning and told me after Byron paid him a visit with Gareth and Winston."

"The twins won't have to be responsible for paying it back?"

"What was so surprising about the visit is Carson said that Byron will require his sons to pay him back every cent, but he wanted the ranchers paid immediately."

Her dad grinned. "Well, I'll be. Never thought I would see something like that. He usually won't admit he's wrong."

"I don't know if he's done that, but when Gareth took the sleeping pills, I think Byron realized going around town insisting his sons were innocent wasn't going to work because they were insisting the opposite."

Abigail put their lunches before them, topped off their

coffee, then left as more customers kept coming into the café.

After he said a blessing, her dad sipped his drink. "Some things don't change. Maggie makes the best cup of coffee in this part of Texas."

"So who have you seen already this morning?" Lucy asked, then took a bite of her hamburger.

"I went over to pay Iva a visit. I hated to hear her health was failing, but she seemed to be in great spirits."

"Ruby's grandmother is like Ben's. Wise with a lot of gumption."

Her father chuckled. "So true. And I'm glad we're going to the Stillwater Ranch tomorrow night for dinner because I want to make sure I see Mamie, too, while I'm here."

"I might not go."

He put his fork down and peered at Lucy. "Why not? She called your mom this morning and said the invitation was for all of us."

"I know. I forgot to tell you all last night."

"That's not like you. I was good friends with her son and she is one I always see when I visit."

Lucy stared at her half-eaten hamburger, no longer hungry. Her stomach clenched like a fist at the thought of going and Ben not being there.

"Are the rumors true about you and Ben seeing each other?"

Lucy yanked her head up. "Who told you that?" She hadn't said anything to her parents about the time she and Ben had been together the past month because she didn't know what to make of it. Her mother would have her married off to him before she got off the phone because she wanted grandchildren.

"Iva. Then when I asked Carson, he told me y'all had been working on the Robin Hoods case together as well as the annual Easter-egg hunt. He implied something was going on."

One look at her father and Lucy did what she always had done growing up—confided in him. "Yes. It didn't start out that way. We just began spending more and more time together. What do you think of Ben?"

"My opinion isn't the important one."

Lucy told her dad about Ben's son and how he was trying to change. "He takes his father role very seriously, which has surprised me."

"Why? He's always cared about others, sometimes when other people didn't."

She thought of Ben with Gareth and even Winston, especially when some of the townsfolk had wanted to railroad the twins.

"I know Ben's daddy wasn't the best example, but there was a time when he wasn't so angry at the world before his back injury and his wife leaving him. Some get stronger under ordeals, but Ben's father wasn't one of them. He even tested my friendship at times."

"I've seen people say they are changing, but they never do. Do you think Ben could? He said when he came out of the coma he knew he couldn't continue going through life like he was."

"And you don't believe him, or is it something else?"

"I don't know. He told me the other night he loved me, but I've always thought Ben didn't want to be in a long-term relationship. When growing up, he certainly avoided them. He might have the record for dating the most women in the county."

"Nope. I did. Before I met your mom, I didn't want

to get married. I thought the worst thing that could happen to me was to be tied down. But that all changed when your mom came along." He patted her hand between them. "So tell me the real reason you don't want to fall in love."

As her father said the last sentence, Lucy realized she'd already fallen in love with Ben. Every time she'd seen him with Cody her feelings had deepened, but when they kissed, he'd sealed it. She twisted her napkin in her lap, balling it in her fist. "I'm afraid to believe he's changed. I can't risk going through the same thing that happened with Jesse. When I first met Jesse a year before we started dating, he always had a different woman on his arm. He loved flirting. As we were getting serious, I believed him when he told me I was the only one for him. Before he'd just been looking for something casual, but now he knew what he wanted—me. Later I discovered he'd been lying to me even then. I felt like such a fool. It got to the point I didn't want to stay and get all those pitying looks."

"I'm glad you came home, and I'm figuring Ben is, too. Why do you take risks in your job but can't in your personal life?"

"It's different."

"How?"

"I won't get hurt as much."

"I remember when you got beat up taking a chance on the job. I have a feeling that hurt quite a bit."

"Not the same."

"Isn't it? Remember what God said about waiting for perfect conditions? Nothing will get done. That's not you. You are a doer. I hope you'll reconsider going to the Stillwater Ranch tomorrow evening."

She couldn't get what her father said to her at lunch out of her mind the rest of the day. It wasn't like her not to face a problem head-on and deal with it. She would go tomorrow evening and hope that Ben was there. They needed to talk.

Ben slanted a glance at Betsy sitting in the front seat of his truck. After going to a short list of places the private investigator had given him in the Dallas/Fort Worth area, he'd finally found her at a church's day care. He might have messed up his chance with Lucy, but at least he'd been able to find Betsy. He'd hated being away from Little Horn and Cody, even for a short time, but it had been worth it when he'd seen the surprise on Betsy's face when she spied him.

"We're almost to Little Horn," Ben said as he passed the welcome sign, remembering his time with Lucy beautifying the bed around the sign. He didn't want it to be over with them. Would he be able to convince her he was a changed man?

"Do you think my cousin will let me see Gareth and Winston?" Betsy swung her attention to Ben, her long ponytail swishing around.

Her hair reminded Ben of Byron's strawberry blond, but that was where the similarity ended with her cousin. When Ben had approached Betsy yesterday at the church where she worked in the day care, he'd spent time watching the eighteen-year-old with the children and made a decision right then and there. "Gareth likes Maddy, and Byron invited her to dinner after church last Sunday. Maddy told me it went well, so yes, I think Byron will let you see the twins." He hoped. But if Byron didn't, he and his family would be there for Betsy.

"Maddy had a crush on Gareth before I left Little Horn. I'm sure this whole situation has been very upsetting to her."

"If you're going to take care of my son, I'd like you to stay at my ranch. We have a big house. But you don't have to. I thought that would help you save some money for your college tuition. I'm still going to see if the Lone Star Cowboy League can give you a scholarship like Tyler had. We can always use good teachers at our school." He was going to make it a priority to start a scholarship fund to go to one youth each year, maybe even talk Byron into helping.

"I've loved working with the kids. Cody sounds adorable."

"He is. He took his first few steps over the weekend, so it won't be long before he's all over the house." Ben turned into the gate at the Stillwater Ranch. "No one knows where I went. I wanted to surprise everyone."

"I never thought anyone in town would be looking for me. My cousin didn't make me feel welcomed at his ranch nor in Little Horn. I had to put distance between us. Six months ago I couldn't have returned. It was too painful."

"Byron is only one person. A lot of people were concerned where you disappeared to." Ben parked next to a SUV, probably Lucy's parents'.

Would she be here, too? He hoped so. They needed to talk. Saturday he hadn't made himself clear. His old life held no appeal to him.

"Ready, Betsy?"

"Who's here?" She pointed toward the SUV.

"The Bensons. They are back for a month and staying with Lucy."

"Is she here, too?"

"I don't know. She was invited, but her job can interfere with her plans." But more likely, the reason would be that he'd told her he loved her.

Betsy carried a duffel bag toward the front porch while Ben grabbed her two pieces of luggage where she packed all her worldly possessions. When he opened the door, the sound of voices came from the living room. He put her suitcases down and gestured her to stay until he went inside.

The first and really only person he saw when he stepped through the entrance was Lucy. Her eyes lit up, and she smiled.

"Where have you been? I was getting worried," Grandma Mamie said, pulling his attention to her.

"I went to the Dallas/Fort Worth area and came back with a surprise. I have it with me now."

Betsy came into the room and stood next to him. "Ben convinced me to return to Little Horn." Her gaze took in the grinning faces but stopped at Maddy's. Tears filled both girls' eyes.

Maddy leaped to her feet and hugged Betsy, both of them now crying. "Thank You, Lord, for bringing Betsy home."

Again drawn to Lucy, Ben looked at her and her eyes were glistening, too, as well as her mom's, Chloe's and Mamie's. There was a spot next to Lucy on the couch, and he took the seat.

She turned toward him. "You found her. Things are definitely looking up. Is she staying?"

"Yep. I gave her a job. She's going to be Cody's new nanny. She belongs here."

"What about Byron?"

"She's family. It's his loss if he doesn't acknowledge that. With the twins probably going to the juvenile detention facility in Austin soon, Betsy and his wife will be all the family he has here." Ben scanned the people in his living room. At the moment Lucy's mother held Cody, but he wiggled, ready to be put down.

Lucy's mother set him on the floor by her feet. Cody crawled to Ben, then pulled himself up to stand next to his legs with his arms raised up.

Ben bent forward and gathered his son into his arms. "Did you miss me, little man?"

Cody reached out, grabbing for Ben's face while jabbering.

"I think he did," Lucy said.

The question Ben really wanted to ask was "Did you miss me, Lucy?" But he would have to bide his time.

Lucy put the last plate in the dishwasher and closed the lid. "Finally we're done."

"You didn't have to help me. You're a guest." Chloe wiped down the counter by the sink. "But I'm glad you did. You've been awfully quiet tonight. Something bothering you? Perhaps connected to Ben? At church on Sunday you two didn't even talk."

"He told me he loved me Saturday night."

"And what did you say?"

"I panicked. I've been under fire before and when he said the L word all I could think about were the reasons he didn't really."

One of Chloe's eyebrows arched. "Oh, and why do you think that?"

"In the past, when has Ben ever been serious about a woman?"

"Never, but there is always a first time." Chloe lounged against the counter, studying Lucy. "You two talked a little earlier."

"Only pleasantries."

"What do you want?"

"I need to make him understand about why I reacted like I did. When we departed on Saturday, Ben was clearly upset."

"That's because I've never told a woman I loved her except my mom and grandmother." Ben leaned against the doorjamb, his arms folded over his chest.

"I think that's my cue to leave." Chloe hurried around Ben and left them alone.

Silence electrified the air.

Ben shoved away from the door, closed it and crossed to Lucy. "So why did you react as if I asked you to drink a vial of poison?"

"You took me by surprise."

"When I said I loved you?"

She nodded, her throat jammed with emotions she'd been wrestling with for the past few days.

"I meant what I said. It wasn't a spur-of-the-moment thing. I've never felt like this before. I've certainly never been in love."

"Are you sure? Maybe what you're feeling is gratitude?"

"For what? Nope. While I was looking for Betsy, all I thought about was you. Somehow I had to make you understand I'm not going back to the man I was. I want to spend the rest of my life with you, but I'll go as slow as you want. If I have to prove to you I mean what I say, I will. One day I'll wear you down."

"I told you about Jesse dating two other women when

we were supposed to be exclusive. What I didn't say was that he'd had a reputation for being a ladies' man, and I believed him when he told me he wasn't that guy any longer. That I was the one for him. The only one."

Ben closed the space between them. "And you were afraid I would be just like him?"

"You used to be like that. You dated a woman for a while, then moved on, never really committing to a relationship."

"The key words are *used to be*. God gave me a wake-up call, and I listened. In all the years you've known me, have I ever gone back on my word?"

"No." His nearness revved her heartbeat, making her mouth go dry.

He pulled her against him and locked his hands behind her back. "I don't ever want to let you go. I want to marry you, and *when* we do, you'll decide what you want to do as far as your job. I'll be here to support your decision. That's why I went to find Betsy. Maddy reminded me she used to babysit for extra money and loved working with children. I wanted to give her a good reason to return to Little Horn. She's going to work and go to the nearby community college in the evening."

She remembered what her father had said about taking a risk. She'd never been a coward before, and she wasn't going to start now. She wound her arms around him. "I love you, Ben. But even more than that. I trust you."

Ben smiled and bent his head toward hers. When he kissed her, she knew she'd made the right decision. Every part of her responded to him as though he was the only other person in the world—and he was for her.

Epilogue

After the wedding party's photos were taken in the church, Lucy entered her reception in the hall with her husband next to her. Dressed in her mother's gown of beaded satin, she had never felt as feminine as she did right now.

Ben paused in the entrance, squeezing her hand. "I didn't realize so many people were here."

"It looks like the whole town."

"You are the sheriff."

When he smiled at her, it warmed her from head to toe. "And you are the president of the Lone Star Cowboy League."

"Never thought I would do something like that, but with Carson gone a lot for his job with the state, it makes sense."

"Just so long as Byron didn't get the position. I'd much prefer working with you in the future." Lucy searched the huge crowd in the large church hall and saw the man under discussion. "He's mellowed some in six months."

"Yeah, wonders never cease. He even told Betsy she

could go with him and his wife to see Gareth and Winston next weekend at the juvenile detention center. Are you ready to mingle with our guests, Mrs. Stillwater?"

Goose bumps raced up her arms when he said her new name. "I see Grady waving to us."

As Ben threaded his way through the townspeople, Amelia snagged Lucy's attention. When she neared her friend, Amelia hugged her and whispered, "I'm thrilled for you. You seemed to float down the aisle."

Lucy laughed. "I hardly remember walking into church, let alone down the aisle. Everyone was a blur except Ben."

"I know what you mean. I was so glad Finn and I had a lot of pictures taken to recall what happened at my own wedding."

When they continued their way through the crowd, guests kept delaying Ben and her. By the time they reached Grady and Chloe, Cody had fallen asleep in his uncle's arms.

"I tried to keep him up until you got here, but he's worn-out. Our Emma conked out halfway through the wedding, according to Grandma. Betsy is going to drive them back to the ranch and put them down for the night. Maddy is going with her to help. Since you two are leaving on your honeymoon after the reception, I thought you might want to say good-night to Cody."

Ben took Cody and nestled him in the crook of his arm. "I'll carry him to the car."

Lucy kissed the little boy's forehead. "I know we'll only be gone a week, but I'm going to miss him and Emma."

"And when you get back, I'll be having my grand opening of the physical therapy clinic." Chloe beamed, her gaze trapped by Grady's. "I'm waiting until you all are back. Without Grady's and Ben's help, the clinic wouldn't have been possible."

"We know firsthand how good you are as a physical therapist," Ben said, Chloe's second-biggest champion, having completely regained his mobility from the mild stroke caused by his head injury.

While Ben started for the exit, Grady pushed the stroller next to his brother. Grady said something to Ben, and they both laughed.

Carson and Ruby joined Lucy and Chloe. "I wasn't sure those two would ever mend their relationship."

Chloe turned toward the couple. "It's hard for them to stay mad at each other when Cody is like a big brother to his baby cousin and won't let anything bad happen to Emma."

Lucy saw Eva and waved at her. "Did you hear Eva and Tyler got a call about a baby up for adoption?"

"Yep. Once Mamie found out, it was probably all over Little Horn within twenty-four hours," Carson said with a laugh.

Ben returned, saw Clint and went to him. After he said something to Olivia's husband, who strode to the exit, Ben headed straight for Carson. "I thought I'd let you know Brandon and Olivia's triplets are in the big elm by the parking lot. I think one of the triplets is stuck up in the tree. Grady is trying to get them down. I told him I would find you and Clint."

In less than five minutes most of the wedding party and guests were outside, trying to figure out how to get Noah down from the very top of the elm. Grady had made it halfway up the tree but had to stop and try to coax him down with words. It wasn't working. Noah clung to the thin branch he had managed to perch himself on. Clint was under the elm, helping down Noah's two brothers, Levi and Caleb. Brandon was the last one to hop from the tree, Carson bear-hugging his nephew.

Lucy saw Olivia's face lose its color and quickly said to Ben, "Do you have your cell phone on you?"

"Yes." He drew it out of his pocket.

She called the volunteer fire department, and Larry promised to be right there with the hook and ladder truck. When she hung up, she looked at Ben.

"And that's why you're the sheriff. You know what to do in an emergency. I hope we don't have to rescue Grady, too."

Twenty minutes later, everyone, including Grady, was out of the elm, as sounds of the cheering crowd filled the air. The kids at the reception were swarming all over the hook and ladder while Larry showed them what it did.

As the crowd slowly headed back inside, Ben grabbed Lucy. "I love you, Mrs. Stillwater. You saved the day."

Blushing, she put her arms around his neck, tugged his head toward her and gave him a kiss that held all the emotions she felt toward this man. Six months ago she'd made the right choice that she knew she would never regret.

* * * * *

Keep reading for an exclusive excerpt of
THE RAIN SPARROW by
New York Times *bestselling author Linda Goodnight.*
Available now from HQN Books!

Dear Readers,

I was excited to write the last book in the Love Inspired continuity series with such great authors. Thanks, Brenda, Leigh, Allie, Carolyne and Deb. You made the process so much easier.

Ben and Lucy's love story was such fun to write. This book was about forgiveness. Ben had trouble forgiving his father and himself for what his anger led him to— not taking life seriously. He thought if he had enough fun he would be happy, but it took being in a coma for weeks to discover he had been so wrong about life, especially about making commitments.

But Ben wasn't the only one with issues. Lucy wasn't sure she could trust a man again, especially a ladies' man like her ex-boyfriend. He made her doubt her judgment. When we start to doubt ourselves, we need to turn to the Lord. He's there to help us through our doubts.

I love hearing from readers. You can contact me at margaretdaley@gmail.com or at PO Box 2074, Tulsa, OK 74101. You can also learn more about my books at www.margaretdaley.com. I have an email newsletter that you can sign up for on my website.

Best wishes,

Margaret Daley

A mystery writer and a shy librarian find love on a dark, stormy night in Honey Ridge, Tennessee...

BARE FEET SOUNDLESS on the cool tile flooring, Carrie moved to a pantry and removed one of Julia's sterling silver French press urns. "We'll have to grind the beans. Julia's a bit of a coffee snob."

"Won't the noise disturb the others?"

Thunder rattled the house. Carrie tilted her head toward the dark, rain-drenched window. "Will it matter?"

"Point taken. You're a lifesaver. What's your name?"

"Carrie Riley." She kept her hands busy and her eyes on the work. The fact that she was ever-so-slightly aware of the stranger with the poet's face in a womanly kind of way gave her a funny tingle. She seldom tingled, and she didn't flirt. She was no good at that kind of thing. Just ask her sisters. "Yours?"

"Hayden Winters."

"Nice to meet you, Hayden." She held up a canister of coffee beans. "Bold?"

"I can be."

She laughed, shocked to think this handsome man might actually be flirting a little. Even if she wasn't. "Bold, it is."

As she'd predicted, the storm noise covered the grinding sound and in fewer than ten minutes, the silver pot's lever was pressed and the coffee was poured. The dark, bold aroma filled the kitchen, a pleasing warmth against the rain-induced chill.

Hayden Winters offered her the first cup, a courteous gesture that made her like him, and then sipped his. "You know your way around a bold roast."

"Former Starbucks barista who loves coffee."

"A kindred spirit. I live on the stuff, especially when I'm working, which I should be doing."

She didn't want him to leave. Not because he was hot—which he was—but because she didn't want to be alone in the storm, and no one else was up. "You work at night?"

"Stormy nights are my favorite."

Which, in her book, meant he was a little off-center. "What do you do?"

He studied her for a moment and, with his expression a peculiar mix of amusement and malevolence, said quietly, matter-of-factly, "I kill people."

REQUEST YOUR FREE BOOKS!

2 FREE INSPIRATIONAL NOVELS
PLUS 2
FREE
MYSTERY GIFTS

EXCLUSIVE
Limited Time Offer

$1.⁵⁰ OFF

New York Times Bestselling Author
LINDA GOODNIGHT
welcomes you back home to
Honey Ridge, Tennessee, with another
beautiful story full of hope, haunting
mystery and the power to win your heart.

THE
RAIN
SPARROW

Available February 23, 2016.
Pick up your copy today!

HQN™

$15.99 U.S./$18.99 CAN.

$1.⁵⁰ OFF the purchase price of THE RAIN SPARROW
by Linda Goodnight.

Offer valid from February 23, 2016, to March 31, 2016.
Redeemable at participating retail outlets. Not redeemable at Barnes & Noble.
Limit one coupon per purchase. Valid in the U.S.A. and Canada only.

52613252

5 65373 00078 6 (8100)0 12117

PHLG0316COUP

Turn your love of reading into
rewards you'll love with
Harlequin My Rewards

**Join for FREE today at
www.HarlequinMyRewards.com**

Earn **FREE BOOKS** of your choice.

Experience **EXCLUSIVE OFFERS** and contests.

Enjoy **BOOK RECOMMENDATIONS**
selected just for you.

PLUS! Sign up now
and get **500** points
right away!

MYR16R